"I can pay my own way."

Macey folded her hand over Cole's, crushing the money between his fingers. "No one said you couldn't. But when someone else wants to do something nice for you, just say thank you."

"Thank you." Heat warmed Cole's neck.

Macey looked at him hesitantly. "Aunt Lynetta asked me to check on Lexi. So if you don't mind me taking a quick peek…"

Grinning, Cole closed the storm door behind her. He nearly bumped into Macey as he turned around.

He grabbed her arms as her hands flew to his shoulders. "Whoa. Sorry about that. I didn't expect you to be so close."

He certainly didn't mind, though.

Being around Macey for the past couple of weeks ignited feelings he'd snuffed out after his ex-wife had left.

But they were friends, and that was all they could be.

The last thing he needed was to fall for the daughter of his uncle's enemy.

No matter how well she fit into their lives.

Heart, home and faith have always been important to **Lisa Jordan**, so writing stories with those elements comes naturally. Happily married for over thirty years to her real-life hero, she and her husband have two grown sons, and they are embracing their new season of grandparenting. Lisa enjoys quality time with her family, reading good books and being creative with friends. Learn more about her and her writing by visiting www.lisajordanbooks.com.

Books by Lisa Jordan

Love Inspired

Visit the Author Profile page at LoveInspired.com.

Rescuing
Her Ranch

Lisa Jordan

LOVE INSPIRED
INSPIRATIONAL ROMANCE

LOVE INSPIRED®

INSPIRATIONAL ROMANCE

Recycling programs for this product may not exist in your area.

ISBN-13: 978-1-335-58553-0

Rescuing Her Ranch

Love Inspired
22 Adelaide St. West, 41st Floor
Toronto, Ontario M5H 4E3, Canada
www.LoveInspired.com

Printed in U.S.A.

Trust in the Lord with all thine heart;
and lean not unto thine own understanding.
In all thy ways acknowledge him,
and he shall direct thy paths.

—Proverbs 3:5–6

For Jeanette and Gabe Walter—
you're NF warriors and such blessings to so many!
May your stories bless others
and change their lives.

Acknowledgments

Lord, may my words glorify You.

My family—Patrick, Scott, Mitchell,
Sarah and Bridget. I love you forever.

Thanks to Jeanne Takenaka and Alena Tauriainen
for brainstorming, texting and calling
when I was feeling overwhelmed by this story.
Thanks to Dana R. Lynn and Christy Miller for
being wonderful sounding boards. Thanks to my
Novel Academy morning sprint crew for daily
prayers and encouragement as I wrote this story.

Thanks to Jeanette Walter, Jen Tezbir,
Dalyn Weller and Jeanne Takenaka for your
willingness to answer my research questions.
Any mistakes are mine.

Thanks to Cynthia Ruchti, my inspiring agent,
and Melissa Endlich, my exceptional editor,
for continually encouraging and inspiring me to
grow as a writer. So thankful you're on my team.
And to the Love Inspired team who works hard
to bring my books to print.

Chapter One

Macey was back where she started.

But this time, instead of standing on Cole Crawford's porch with tears streaking her makeup while blasting him for the humiliation he caused her, she was offering her help.

Only because Everly, her baby sister, had begged her.

Otherwise, she'd still be ignoring Cole like she'd been doing for the past decade.

With her career—and quite possibly her reputation—ruined, Macey returned home. Disgrace drove her out of Denver where she'd been a nanny for the Crane family for the past six years—since graduating college with her degree in early childhood education.

Maybe she should've waited until morning to leave the city instead of driving through the mountains, going thirty miles an hour while the blizzard howled and swirled around her.

But she couldn't stay a minute longer. Her broken heart pined for the security of home where no one could take advantage of her.

With her car loaded down with nearly everything

she owned and nowhere else to go, failure and shame chased her all the way back to Stone River, the cattle ranch nestled in the valley of the San Juan Mountains in southwestern Colorado that had been in her family for three generations.

Now, with an icy wind sliding down her back, Macey scuffed her boots on the snow-covered welcome mat. She glanced over her shoulder and nearly sprinted back to her still-warm car parked in front of Cole's stone-face condo.

But she couldn't do that. She'd given her word.

If she wasn't jobless and slightly desperate at the moment, she wouldn't have given in to Everly's pleading.

Tightening the hold on her tote bag, she drew in a steadying breath, released it slowly, then pressed the doorbell.

The oak door trimmed in white opened, and Macey forced her jaws to stay closed.

The tall, lanky kid with braces from her childhood had grown into a broad-shouldered man who filled the doorway with his presence. Worn jeans did little to disguise his muscular legs. His hoodie stretched over his broad shoulders as he held a little girl with blond curls in his arms. His square jaw sported a darkened shadow that couldn't conceal the dimple in his left cheek. His dirty-blond hair had darkened to a rich brown. About the only thing unchanged were his eyes. They were still as blue as the Colorado sky.

"Cole?"

A smile stretched across his face, revealing even white teeth. He stepped back and opened the door wider. "Macey Stone. Hey. Come in."

She moved into the foyer, and he closed the door behind her. The heated interior warmed her cold cheeks as she breathed in the scent of freshly brewed coffee in the air.

He shifted the little girl, who had the same blue eyes as her daddy, to his other arm. "I have to admit, I was a bit surprised when Everly called first thing this morning to say she couldn't care for Lexi but that you agreed to fill in for her. I didn't know you'd returned to Aspen Ridge."

Macey tugged off her gloves and stuffed them in her pockets. "It was a last-minute decision. Did she tell you why she couldn't come?"

He nodded, his jaw tight. "Yes, and I hope the interview goes well."

"If Ev's offered the long-term substitute job at Aspen Ridge Elementary, that will get her foot in the door for a full-time position next year."

"While I'm happy for her, it also means I may be looking for a new caregiver for my Lexi Lou." He blew kisses on the child's neck, causing her to giggle.

Lexi cupped Cole's face. "Daddy, you're so silly. I'm not Lexi Lou. I'm Lexi Jane."

Cole thunked the heel of his hand against his forehead. "Oh, that's right. My mistake."

The little girl giggled again, her eyes never leaving Macey.

"Everly said you were a nanny in Denver."

"Yes, I was. For nearly six years." A rush of tears pooled in Macey's eyes, and she forced them back. She wasn't about to have an emotional breakdown in front of Cole and his daughter.

"Was? You're not any longer?"

"No. Things ended suddenly last night." She rubbed

her arms to erase the feel of Mr. Crane's tightening hold on her skin.

He frowned. "So if things ended last night, then that means you must've driven through the mountains in the blizzard to get home. We're like five hours from Denver. When did you sleep?"

"It was about seven hours, since visibility wasn't all that great. I arrived at the ranch around four this morning and managed to get three solid hours of sleep before Everly woke me up."

"You must've wanted to get home pretty quickly."

"You have no idea." Not ready to talk about what drove her out of Denver and away from the three children she loved like her own, Macey pressed a smile in place. She turned to Lexi and held out her hand. "Hi, Lexi Jane. My name is Macey, and I'm Everly's sister."

The little girl's eyes widened as she scrambled out of her father's arms. She stood in front of Macey. "You got my name right." Then she turned to Cole, small hands on her hips. "See, Daddy, she knows my name. Maybe she can teach you."

Cole shot them a lopsided grin. "That's not a bad idea."

Macey crouched in front of Lexi. "Everly has an appointment today. Do you mind if I stay with you while your daddy goes to work?"

Lexi leaned against Cole's legs as her bottom lip popped out. "But Everly and I were going to make cookies today. Chocolate chip. Daddy's favorite."

"Well, Everly remembered and gave me the ingredients to make cookies with you." Macey pulled a package of chocolate chips from her oversize shoulder tote and showed it to Lexi. "See?"

Lexi danced in a circle and jumped up and down. Then she reached for Macey's hand and waved to Cole. "Bye, Daddy. You can go to work now. Macey and I are gonna bake cookies."

Cole laughed, a sound that rattled Macey's locked memory bank. "Well, that was easier than I thought."

"Cookies work wonders."

"Not just the cookies." He studied her a moment, then gripped the back of his neck. "Listen, Mace, I know we haven't talked in a while—"

"A while? It's been ten years." She held up a hand. "To be honest, I don't have the energy to rehash the past right now."

A muscle jumped in the side of his jaw, and he gave her a single nod. "Fair enough."

He opened a door and grabbed a hanger. "Give me your coat and I'll hang it up for you."

She shrugged out of her red wool coat, unwrapped her knitted gray cashmere scarf and handed both to him. "Thanks."

After hanging her coat in the closet, he waved her into the house. "Come in, and I'll share Lexi's routine with you."

She toed off her winter boots, lining them up in the corner by the closet, then followed him into a large open room painted off-white. She dug her socked toes into the tan carpeting. "Nice place."

Morning sunlight poured through floor-to-ceiling windows that offered a gorgeous view of the river snaking through Aspen Ridge, the small ranching community, into the base of the San Juan Mountains.

A dark leather couch with matching recliner had been angled in front of the large flat-screen TV. Lexi's table and chairs, playhouse and toy box sat in the corner next to a child-sized purple recliner and overflowing bookshelf.

A professional portrait of Cole holding Lexi as an infant hung on the wall next to the TV. No other pictures, plants, throw pillows, knickknacks or homey touches adorned the room. Nothing feminine or any evidence of a wife. And the place was spotless.

Cole grabbed a notebook off the coffee table in front of the couch. "This is what Everly and I use to share information about Lexi. She lets me know how Lexi's day has gone, and I communicate about her nights." He flipped it open. "Here's her daily routine. She does better with a schedule. I'm not sure how much Everly's told you about Lexi…"

"To be honest, very little. She takes confidentiality seriously. All I knew was she was caring for a little girl with a medical condition. Until this morning, I didn't know she was your child."

"And you still came." Cole eyed the little girl sitting on the couch with a book next to a stuffed pony. "Lexi has neurofibromatosis. Or NF1 for short. Basically, benign tumors form on nerve tissue in her body. And each case is different. For Lexi, though, it's affecting her hearing, which is also affecting her learning."

"She's so happy and upbeat."

"She is. For the most part. Like any kid, she has her moments."

Macey glanced at Cole's left hand and found it bare. "Everly mentioned you're no longer married."

He shook his head and gripped the back of his neck. "My ex and I were married only a couple of months when she became pregnant. She didn't want kids right away, and we fought about it. She left us the day after Lexi was born. She signed away her parental rights, and I was served with divorce papers the day after I brought Lexi home from the hospital. So, we've been on our own from the very beginning."

"I'm so sorry. That must've been tough." Her instinct was to wrap her arms around him, but she stayed where she was.

Even though the decade-old anger had faded, she and Cole weren't exactly friends anymore.

He lifted a shoulder. "It is what it is. I can't change the past. I'm just doing what I can to be the best father she deserves. I'll do whatever it takes to give her what she needs."

Her phone vibrated in her back pocket. She pulled it out and saw Everly's picture on her screen. "Excuse me a second." She turned away from Cole and Lexi. "Hello?"

"Mace, I got it! Mrs. Penley hired me for the long-term sub job." Everly squealed so loudly that Macey had to pull the phone away from her ear.

"Ev, that's great. Congratulations." Macey forced joy into her voice, but her stomach burned, just knowing what Everly planned to ask her.

"Thanks. I know it's a lot to ask and you just got home, but I don't suppose you'd consider caring for Lexi until Cole can find someone more permanent. She's a super sweet kid, and I really hate to leave him in a lurch, but I really want to take this job. Say yes, please?"

Even though Cole had taken Lexi into the kitchen, she was sure he could hear her side of the conversation.

"Can we talk about this later? Preferably after I've had more sleep and time for my brain cells to kick in."

Everly remained silent for a moment. "Well, Mrs. Penley asked if I could start tomorrow. I need to handle some paperwork and take a tour of the school."

Macey swallowed a sigh. "Ev, I haven't even taken care of Lexi yet. I don't even know if we'll get along."

"That's silly, and you know it. Of course, she's going to like you. Everyone does."

Not everyone.

"Please, Macey, I wouldn't ask if this weren't so important. We're talking about my teaching future. You know how hard I've worked for this." The pleading in her sister's voice tugged at Macey.

What could she say? Macey would've realigned the planets for Everly if she'd been asked. Her baby sister had to overcome a lot of obstacles in her twenty-two years, and Macey didn't want to stand in the way of her dream. But to see Cole on a daily basis...was she up for that?

She glanced at the single father brushing his daughter's hair into a ponytail while Lexi stood on a stool at the counter, and her heart softened. "Okay, yeah, fine. I'll talk to Cole and see what he thinks. But you owe me. Big time."

Everly squealed again. "Yes! Anything you want. Thankyouthankyouthankyou."

Before she could respond, the line went silent in her ear. Macey tossed her phone from hand to hand, then walked into the kitchen.

With her hair pulled back, Lexi now spread peanut butter on a slice of bread. "Look, Macey, I'm making Daddy's lunch."

"You're doing a great job." She turned to Cole. "Not sure how much you heard."

Holding a jar of homemade jam, he closed the fridge, then leaned against the counter. "Enough to know I'm losing your sister as my daughter's caregiver."

Macey nodded, dropped her gaze to her darkened screen, then looked back at Cole. "She asked if I'd be willing to fill in until you could find someone more permanent."

He straightened, and his eyebrows lifted. "Oh, really? How do you feel about that?"

Macey pocketed her phone, then shrugged. "Lexi doesn't know me. We may not be a good fit."

Cole shot her a half smile. "I've known your family nearly all my life. Your brothers are my closest friends. Plus, I trust your sister. If she believes you can do this, then I do too. Besides, Lex is pretty easygoing. She gets along with most everyone."

Pressing her back against the sink, Macey ran a thumb and forefinger over her gritty eyes. "I've been home only a few hours, and my plate is filling already."

Cole touched her elbow. "Hey, what's going on?"

"Bear called yesterday. Dad passed out in the pasture after lunch, and Bear found him facedown in the snow. They called 911 and rushed him to the hospital. The doctors are running tests, and they suspect pneumonia. Mom spent most of the night by his side. When I came downstairs this morning, I found her at the table with this overwhelmed look on her face. She's been planning the annual Stone River Sweetheart Ball. But now with Dad sick, she's stressed about getting everything done on time. Since I'll be home for a while, she asked if I'd consider taking over."

Macey didn't share about the flashbacks she had to

the humiliating prom she'd planned in painstaking detail only be left as the laughingstock in the community.

"Wow, Mace. I had no idea. I'm sorry to hear about your dad. The Sweetheart Ball is such a great fundraiser." He dragged a hand over his face. "Listen, don't worry about Lexi. I'll come up with a different solution. Maybe my cousin Piper can help me out."

Macey should've felt relief at being freed from caring for Lexi, but the tightness in Cole's jaw and the deepening lines around his mouth made her think finding someone to care for his daughter was going to be harder than she imagined. Her shoulders sagged as she shook her head. "No, don't do that. I'll take care of her until you can find a permanent provider for her."

Cole's head jerked up and his eyes brightened. "You have no idea what that means to me. Without much of a family to fall back on, I wasn't quite sure what I was going to do. But if you're sure…"

She nodded, but the voice in her head urged her to grab her coat and run back to her car. But after what had happened last night, she wasn't sure about anything right now, especially on such little sleep.

Cole slid the sandwich Lexi made into a plastic baggie and dropped it in his lunch box. Then he gripped the edge of the counter. "After Mom died suddenly of that heart defect when I was a freshman, your family's charity event has always been important to me." He made a face. "Listen, since you're willing to help me out until I can find a permanent solution for Lexi's care, then the least I can do is give you a hand with organizing the Sweetheart Ball."

She waved away his words. "You don't have to do that. You have more than enough to keep you busy."

"I want to."

"I don't know, Cole."

He reached for her hand. "Listen, Macey. I was a jerk at our prom, and I've regretted screwing up our friendship for the past ten years. I'm so sorry I stood by while Celeste humiliated you. I cared more about being accepted than standing up for my best friend. Let me prove I'm not that same punk, and you can trust me again."

Macey rubbed a hand across her forehead and over her tired eyes. She smothered a yawn, then nodded. "Okay, let's talk more when you get home. What time should I expect you?"

"Probably around five. If something changes, I'll let you know. Will that be a problem?"

Macey shook her head.

He glanced at his watch and headed to the living room. "I'm already late, and my uncle's going to be furious. We'll talk more tonight. Thank you, Macey. I mean it."

As he headed out the door, Macey allowed his words to linger between them. She wanted to lean into them, to know he'd be there for her. But their years of friendship had been destroyed by a single humiliating act that brought her shame when his voice could have changed everything.

Even though she wanted nothing more than to return to the safety of Stone River, Macey remained in Cole's living room, determined to prove she wasn't a failure. After all, no matter how she felt about Cole, his sweet daughter didn't need to suffer.

Mom's words from earlier drifted into her head— maybe God brought her home for a reason.

While she tried to determine her purpose for the future, she'd guard her heart because the last thing she needed was to fall for Cole again, only to have him break it once more.

Cole had been given a second chance for redemption, and he wasn't about to waste it. He still couldn't believe Macey Stone was back in town and she'd offered to care for his daughter.

He certainly didn't deserve her kindness, especially after the way he'd treated her all those years ago. Only an idiot would've let a friend like her storm out of his life.

Now he'd make amends for the humiliating prom fiasco and rekindle their friendship.

Truth was, he missed her. He hadn't realized how much until he opened his door and found her standing on his snow-covered porch.

Even though he was a regular visitor at Stone River Ranch, Macey had always managed to sneak away while visiting her family before he could see her.

Time hadn't diminished her beauty. If anything, it enhanced it. Her chestnut-brown hair still fell in light waves around her shoulders. And those expressive brown eyes couldn't hide her emotions.

Thumbing through his emails on his phone, Cole opened the door to the mobile office at the Riverside Condos construction site and ducked inside to escape the cold biting at his neck.

"About time you showed up."

Cole's head jerked up and his gut tightened. Wallace Crawford, his uncle and his boss, sat at Cole's desk with his booted feet on the oversize desk calendar.

"Yeah, sorry about that. I had a last-minute child-care issue." Cole set his insulated travel mug on the L-shaped desk and dropped his lunch made by Lexi in the mini fridge tucked under the microwave.

Wallace pushed to his feet and grabbed his black cowboy hat off the coatrack behind Cole's desk chair. "Don't get too comfortable. We have a meeting."

"A meeting with whom?" Cole pulled out his phone and tapped on his calendar app but didn't find anything scheduled.

"Aspen Ridge City Council."

"For what?"

"I've been talking with Mayor Cobb about building a strip mall, and he thinks it will be a good boost to the local economy."

Cole frowned. "A strip mall? Where?"

"Off the highway exit that leads into town."

Cole turned to the framed map of Aspen Ridge hanging above the drafting table. He tapped the exit Wallace referenced. "But that's Stone River Ranch property."

Wallace grinned, looking more like a wolf hunting prey. "Exactly. The city council sent out a letter of intent. They offered to purchase a portion of the property."

"Which part?"

"Old Man Stone's crumbling homestead on the southwestern section of the ranch."

"South Bend?" The southern portion of the ranch the Stones referred to as South Bend where Deacon Stone's parents had lived until their unexpected death ten years ago. "Deacon refused to sell their land when you made an offer after his parents had been killed by that drunk driver."

Wallace lifted a shoulder. "Yeah, so? I have it on

good authority that the Stones are hurting for money. My—I mean, the council's offer could help them stay in the black and it gives me…us the land we need for the project."

"Why that land? And why a strip mall? We're still finishing up the Riverside Condos project. Let me do some research for other parcels that may work better."

"I don't want to look at other properties. The council wants this land. If the Stones refuse to sell, then they can acquire it through eminent domain. And they want you to be project manager."

"The council wants me? Or *you* want me to do your bidding?" Cole gripped the back of his chair and shook his head. "No way. I can't. Barrett and Wyatt Stone are my best friends. Deacon and Nora and Deacon's sister Lynetta helped my mom more times than I can count when she got sick. I can't do that to them. Not to mention, it would be a conflict of interest."

Wallace hooked his thumbs around his belt loops, his fingers framing his decades-old rodeo belt buckle. "Let's sweeten the pot a little, shall we? After your mother's heart gave out, I took you in. Remember the college education I paid for? And that condo where you live? And let's not forget about the medical insurance you need for that little brat of yours. Specialists and those fancy hearing aids don't come cheap. So I'd say you owe me. Pay me back by getting the Stones to sell. Or look for another job…and a new place to live. The choice is yours." Cole clenched his jaw and fought back the words blistering his tongue.

Some choice.

Family meant nothing to Wallace. Something Cole

learned years ago when family services had forced him to live with his last surviving adult relative.

Wallace had Cole backed into a corner and by the smirk on his face, he knew it.

Since graduating college six years ago, Cole worked for his uncle, saving as much as possible so he could reimburse him and be released from the debt hanging over his head.

Not that the guy even needed the money, but Cole didn't want to owe anyone.

"And just so you don't think I'm lacking a heart— get them to sign and you can be the new CEO of my Durango area office. I need someone with smarts to oversee the operations there so I can spend more time on my ranch in Montana. You'll receive a raise, better benefits and I may even throw in a company car."

Coming from anyone else, Cole would've jumped at the opportunity being offered. But with his uncle, everything came with a price. Question was—could Cole pay it and still live with himself?

If it weren't for Lexi, Cole would've walked out the door at that very moment without hesitation. But he'd do anything to provide his daughter with the best care possible, even if it meant selling his soul to someone like his uncle.

Cole scrubbed a hand over his face. "I'll do what I can to get the Stones to sell, but no promises. And we do this by the book."

His uncle clapped him on the back. "You're such a Boy Scout. Stick with me, son, and you'll see how business is really done."

Before Cole could respond he wasn't Wallace's son,

nor did he want to do business the way his uncle did, Wallace stalked out of the trailer.

Grabbing his mug, Cole followed behind, feeling like a jerk. If he talked to Bear and Wyatt and told them about Wallace's land scheme, maybe they'd be little more understanding.

He wouldn't be surprised, though, if they shut him out the way Macey had. And rightly so.

Somehow, he needed to find a way to make this work without hurting those he cared about.

Chapter Two

Macey wanted nothing more than a hot meal and a pillow for her head.

If today was anything to go by, caring for Lexi would be a dream job. She'd been surprised when Cole arrived home earlier than the five o'clock time she'd been told to expect, but even though she'd enjoyed her time with his daughter, she didn't mind a shorter day.

Fatigue settled in her bones like a long-term guest. She hadn't gone without sleep like that since cramming for finals in college. Not even the nights she paced the nursery when little Jaxson Crane screamed due to colic while his mother slept peacefully.

She wondered how Jayden, Jenna and Jaxson were doing without her.

When her defenses were down throughout the day, the three charges had crept into her thoughts. What had Tricia and Derek told their children about Macey's sudden departure?

If only she could've said goodbye. Maybe it wouldn't have hurt so much.

Doubtful.

Nothing could erase the betrayal that buried her trust.

Shutting her eyes couldn't drown out Tricia screaming at her when she discovered her husband in the living room…and in Macey's arms. She'd refused to listen to Macey's cries of innocence as she was ordered to pack and leave, especially when Derek claimed Macey had thrown herself at him.

Never again would she allow anyone to take advantage of her.

For now she was safe. No one would hurt her while she was surrounded by her family.

Pulling in the driveway, Macey shut off the engine and exited the warmth of her car. She headed for the timber-and-stone ranch house, looking forward to climbing the stairs and falling into bed, even if it wasn't even dark yet.

Behind her, a deep woof coupled with a low growl startled her. She jumped and whirled around.

Dakota, or Kota for short, her brother's English shepherd bounded up the steps and sniffed around her boots. His tail wagged as he looked up at her. Macey dropped to her knees, snow and cold seeping into her jeans. She flung her arms around the aging dog. "Hey, Kota. How's it going, boy?"

Kota sniffed Macey, his tail picking up speed. He licked Macey's cheek. She laughed and tried to catch herself so she didn't fall backward.

"Hey, there. No one's home. Can I help you with something?"

At the sound of the deep voice, Macey pushed to her feet and turned. With one hand cupping Kota's head, she jangled the keys still in her gloved hand. "Good thing I have a key."

Barrett, nicknamed Bear by the family, her fraternal twin brother, younger by two minutes, stood on the sidewalk with a coiled rope in his gloved hands. Brown eyes like hers lit up as a smile transformed his stern features. "Hey, Mace. Wyatt mentioned you were back. Sorry I wasn't around this morning to welcome you home."

"Hey, Bear." She lifted a hand and smiled. "No worries. You were busy."

His breath visible in the freezing temperature, he pushed up the brim of his dusty chocolate-colored cowboy hat to reveal more of his tanned face.

Macey pressed a hip against one of the wooden posts of the covered front porch. "Mom's at the hospital, I take it?"

He shook his head. "Actually, Norman Fowler's office."

Straightening, Macey frowned. "Grandma and Grandpa's attorney? Why?"

Bear rubbed the back of his gloved hand across his forehead. "There's been a…development with the ranch."

"What sort of development?"

"After you and Everly left, we received a letter of intent. Supposedly the Aspen Ridge City Council wants to purchase a portion of the land to build a strip mall." Lines bracketing her brother's mouth deepened.

"A strip mall? Why? What part of the ranch?"

"South Bend."

Macey's shoulders sagged as she rested an elbow against the post and cupped her head. "Grandma and Grandpa's property? You can't be serious."

"As a heart attack." He dropped the rope on the porch. "If we don't agree and sign, then they will claim condemnation and take possession. They plan to tear it all down."

"How can they do that?"

"Through eminent domain. With South Bend being closest to town and the highway, they feel it will drive traffic into Aspen Ridge and help the economy. Or so they claim."

"But…" Macey shook her head. The rest of her words remained unspoken. Growing up, she'd taken many horseback rides across the pastures of the original homestead and visited the waterfalls as her grandfather taught her how to use his camera. She'd always said South Bend was her favorite place on earth. Even though nothing was in writing, Grandpa had said it would be hers one day.

Was that not meant to be?

Bear lifted his hat and dragged his hand through his dark brown hair, which was in need of a cut. "After receiving the letter, Mom called Fowler's office and set up an appointment."

"She went alone?" Macey tried to keep the accusatory tone out of her voice, but Bear's raised eyebrow showed she hadn't quite succeeded.

Shaking his head, he laughed. "Like Mom needs any one of us to protect her. The woman's fierce, especially when anyone messes with the family. She wanted to get some facts before she talked to Dad. Besides, Wyatt's with her."

Macey gave Kota a final pat, then closed her fingers around her keys once more. "I'm going to Fowler's office to see what's going on. There has to be a way to protect what's ours."

As she headed down the steps and brushed past him, he caught her elbow. "Hey."

"What?"

His eyes crinkled in the corners as his lips lifted into a half smile. "I'm glad you're home. You look good."

A flash of tears warmed her eyes. Blinking rapidly, she smiled through the haze, then pulled him in for an impulsive hug, breathing in the long-familiar scents of hay, horses and Colorado fresh air. "Thanks, Bear. You look good too. I'm sorry you lost your appeal with the rodeo association."

He stepped back and lifted a shoulder. "It is what it is. Until that mess is settled, there's not much I can do but work the ranch."

But she didn't miss the shadow that passed over his eyes and spoke louder than his words.

As much as she hurt for him and could relate to the false accusations, she had faith he'd work it out. He always did.

She climbed back into her car, then steered around the horseshoe drive lined with tall aspens blanketed with snow, their leafless branches scratching the late afternoon sky puffed with clouds.

Snow drifted against the posts of the fenced pastures. In a few months, lavender and white columbines and vibrant red Alpine paintbrushes would color the grass. Sunshine reflected off the acres of white pastures, pristine and untouched by cattle or wildlife.

The Stone River Ranch arched sign threw a shadow over the hood of the car as she drove through the gate. The ranch house shrunk in her rearview.

As she headed south toward Aspen Ridge, smoky gray mountains crowned with white snowcaps provided a majestic backdrop for the small ranching community that had been settled over two hundred years ago by her ancestors.

Her fingers tightened on the steering wheel as she turned into town, passing the brown-and-white Welcome to Aspen Ridge sign.

Netta's Diner, which had belonged to her grandparents and now her aunt, sat on the corner of Pine Avenue and Main. With its cheery yellow siding, and matching rockers dusted with snow lining the covered wooden porch, the place invited guests to step inside for a home-style meal.

Macey parked in front of the attorney's office across the street from the diner, then stamped the snow and slush off her boots on the rug in front of the door. She hurried inside, the warm office smelling of cinnamon and coffee, and offering relief from the single digit January temperature, despite the late afternoon sunshine.

Allison Brewster, one of Macey's friends from high school and Mr. Fowler's granddaughter, sat at the reception desk. She looked up with a ready smile on her face, then her blue eyes widened. Squealing, she raced around the desk, her arms flailing in the air. "Macey, your mom mentioned you'd come back home. I planned to give you a call after work."

Macey hugged her friend, then looked down at Allison's oversize sweater stretched over her rounded stomach. "How are you feeling? How's this little one doing?"

Allison smiled and cradled her belly. "We're both healthy and strong. No morning sickness. Apparently, third time's a charm."

At twenty-eight, Macey wasn't even close to being married, let alone pregnant with her third child. But Allison had been more than happy to settle in Aspen Ridge after marrying her high school sweetheart.

Allison jerked her head toward the closed door to the right of her desk. "I'm assuming you're here to be with your family?"

Macey tightened her hand on her oversize purse. "I was hoping to join them, if possible."

"Sure, I don't see why not." She moved to the door and tapped before sticking her head inside. "Excuse me, but there's someone else to join your meeting."

Macey stepped into the office filled with heavy, wooden furniture and books on the floor-to-ceiling bookcases. The room smelled of paper, lemon oil and a faint lingering scent of the pipe tobacco that Mr. Fowler favored when no one was around.

Macey's mother turned in her chair and waved her into the office. She patted the empty seat next to hers. "Macey, come in. We're just about to get started."

She sat and a strong arm slid around her shoulders. Macey looked into the blue eyes of her younger brother, Wyatt. He grinned, looking so much like their dad. "Hey, sis."

He'd been a lanky teen, but six years in the Marine Corps filled out his shoulders. Even though he had been discharged two years ago after his wife died in child-birth, his hair was still cut to military regulation.

She gave him a one-armed side hug, the side of her head brushing against his blue-and-black plaid flannel shirt. "Hey, baby brother. It's so great to see again. Bear said you guys were here. I came to see what was going on."

Mr. Fowler cleared his throat. Dressed in a dark blue suit, his balding white hair neatly trimmed, he stood behind his desk, fingertips pressed against the polished wood. His eyebrows lifted, wrinkling his forehead. "Ms. Stone, it's been a while. You look well."

Macey lifted her chin and gave the man a nod. "Thank you, Mr. Fowler. As do you."

Behind her, the hardwood floor creaked, and Macey turned. Her eyes widened. "Cole? What are *you* doing here?"

Instead of wearing jeans and the olive-colored hoodie from that morning, Cole was now dressed in a light gray suit that fit him well, polished black cowboy boots and a red-patterned tie.

He pocketed his hands as his lips thinned. "I'm the project manager, working with the city council and Crawford Developments, overseeing this process."

"Crawford Developments as in the company your uncle owns?" At his nod, Macey glanced between her mother, brother and Cole. "What process are you referring to?"

Mr. Fowler cleared his throat and tugged on the sleeves of his suit jacket. "Maybe we should return to our conversation and fill Macey in on the details."

Macey's stomach tightened again.

Mr. Fowler explained the letter of intent from the city council outlining their desire to buy the southern portion of the ranch to build a strip mall.

Even though Bear had warned her, Macey still felt her face paling as she turned to her mother and Wyatt. "Please tell me this is some sort of joke. You're not going to allow this, are you?"

Wyatt reached for Macey's fisted hands. "Mace, we may not have a choice."

"Of course, we have a choice. They can't just take our property."

Mr. Fowler cleared his throat once again, the sound grating on Macey's fatigued nerves. "Macey, are you aware of eminent domain?"

She lifted a shoulder. "Bear mentioned it, but I don't understand the details."

"If your family chooses not to sell, then the local government is claiming eminent domain to access your family's property for the strip mall. They will purchase the land at a fair market value."

"But what does that mean, exactly?"

"The local government has the power to take private land for public use. In this case, the Aspen Ridge City Council will be working with Crawford Developments. They are willing to pursue partial taking, meaning they don't want the whole ranch—just a portion of property from your family. Both parties have the right to obtain their own appraisals of the property in question. Once those appraisals have been exchanged, we'll enter negotiations. If the two parties can't reach an agreement, then the city council will send out a final offer. If your family refuses that offer, then the local government will go through the courts to take the property. Your family will still receive just compensation."

Macey's eyes darted between her family, Cole and Mr. Fowler. "But that property has been in our family for over two hundred years. And now we're supposed to sit back and say yes?" Without waiting for an answer, she turned to her mother. "What did Dad say about this?"

"He doesn't know yet." Mom picked up the pen on

the table in front of her and twisted it between her fingers. "Once we have all the facts, I'll talk to your father."

Wyatt stood and rounded the table, putting his large hands on her shoulders. "Macey, Dad's not doing so well right now."

Macey swiveled in her seat and looked up at him. Her fingers tightened on the back of the chair. "I thought he had pneumonia. You mean it could be more than that?"

He nodded, lines deepening in his forehead. "They're still trying to find the cause of his high fever, but now his organs are shutting down."

"Shutting down? Why didn't you say something sooner? We should be at the hospital, not at the attorney's office trying to protect our property." She cradled her forehead, then lifted her chin and directed her attention to Cole. "Does your uncle know my father is in the hospital and unable to fight this? Or was that part of his plan? And did you know about this when I agreed to care for your daughter?"

Cole's jaw tightened as he held up a hand. "Macey, I know what this looks like, but I promise you—I did not know about this when you offered to care for Lexi. This is business. The city council isn't trying to take your family's entire ranch. They're offering to buy a small portion. And your family will be paid fair market value for it."

"So I've heard about three times now. But you know what? To you, it may be business, but to me—" she waved a finger between her mother, her brother and herself "—to us, it's personal. And we will do whatever we can to prevent you, your uncle, the city council, or anyone else from taking what is ours."

Head pounding and eyes gritty, Macey wanted

nothing more than to find a bed and a pillow, but she couldn't rest right now. They needed to come up with a plan. To rally together and protect what was theirs.

Still feeling the sting from being unfairly terminated, Macey wasn't about to let someone else take advantage of any of them, even if it meant losing another job.

How was he going to get out of this mess and still meet Lexi's needs?

Somehow, Cole needed to convince the Stone family to sell their property to the council.

Not only would the strip mall offer more jobs and economic opportunities to Aspen Ridge, but the success of the sale would enable Cole to provide better opportunities for his daughter. With the incentives Wallace dangled in front of him, Cole needed to do whatever it took to ensure his daughter received the best care possible.

Then money wouldn't be a constant issue.

No way would he allow history to repeat itself.

Growing up as the only child of a widowed, overworked single mother who'd preached they were responsible for themselves and charity wasn't an option, Cole had fought hard to make his own way in the world. The last thing he wanted was for Lexi to know the gnaw of hunger in her belly or the shame of seeing her toes sticking out of worn shoes.

His cell phone buzzed with an incoming text. He reached for it and read the words from his cousin Piper: On our way up.

Cole glanced at his smart watch. How was it six o'clock already?

When Cole learned about the Stones' meeting with

Norman Fowler, he'd left work early and asked Piper to care for Lexi until his meeting with the Stones was over.

He'd been naive to think Macey wouldn't have shown up at Fowler's office. The Stones stuck together. Like a real family should.

Her accusations from earlier still echoed in his head, but he needed to put that out of his mind. At least for now.

Even though he could work for another three hours, Cole forced himself to shut down his laptop. The rest would have to wait until tomorrow. He needed to go home and spend the evening with Lexi. If he had time and a shred of mental energy, maybe he'd do more work after tucking her into bed.

His office door opened as he slipped his laptop and the rest of his paperwork in his backpack.

"Daddy!" His daughter flew across the room and into his arms. "I missed you."

"I missed you too, peanut." He wrapped her in a hug and planted a kiss on top of her curly blond head.

She cupped his cheeks and stared at him with those bright blue eyes inherited from her mother. "Can we get pancakes now?"

"Sure thing. Let me gather my stuff, and we'll get out of here." With her gathered in his arms, Cole pocketed his phone, then flung the strap of his backpack over his shoulder, knocking his worn Colorado Rockies ball cap off the corner of his desk that his dad had bought him after they'd gone to a baseball game together. Cole put it back where it belonged. Assured his work area was spotless, he turned to his cousin who waited patiently near the door.

"Thanks for keeping her, Piper. I appreciate the last-minute fill-in while I attended that meeting."

"Hey, when you own your business, you can make your own hours." She linked her arm through his. "Even though Macey's helping you out, you need to make time to find a full-time nanny or consider enrolling Lexi in a preschool program now that she's four."

"She's on the list for Stepping Stones Learning Center's fall program."

"Good. You can pay me by taking Avery and me to dinner."

He admired his cousin's drive. Pregnant at seventeen and forced out on her own, Piper had cleaned houses to support herself. Once she turned eighteen, she and Ryland Healy had gotten married and welcomed their daughter, Avery, a week later. After Ry's tragic death, Piper put herself through college, earning her degree in business administration, while still running her house-cleaning business, The Clean Bee, and caring for her daughter.

Now her thriving business had a handful of employees, and she was the most sought-after housecleaning and organizational business in the area.

How could Cole not admire her spunk and tenacity?

"Sounds good. Let's eat at the diner. Lexi loves Lynetta's pancakes."

"Sure thing. I need to pick up Avery from dance class, then we'll meet you there."

They stepped outside, and Cole sucked in a breath as the brisk winds pinched their cheeks. He drew Lexi closer to his chest and hurried to his truck parked behind the office. He put Lexi down, then transferred Lexi's car seat from Piper's car into his. He set his backpack on the floor, locked the door and pocketed his keys. Cole reached for Lexi's hand. "Come on, squirt. Let's go grab a booth at Netta's where it's warm."

They crossed the street. Cole opened the door of the diner and followed his daughter inside. The warmth of the room reheated their cheeks as he inhaled the scents of burgers and fries hanging in the air. Dishes clattering in the kitchen behind the breakfast counter competed with the conversations buzzing in the full dining room.

They slid into a red booth near the front. He set his phone facedown on the table, then pulled Lexi's coloring book and crayons from her backpack. He shrugged out of his wool overcoat and helped Lexi out of her pink puffy jacket and matching hat.

The door opened again, and Cole looked up, expecting to see Piper and Avery. Instead, Macey Stone stepped inside.

She rubbed her mittened hands together. A gray knitted hat covered her dark hair and a matching scarf wound around her neck. Her red wool coat parted, giving a hint of a light blue sweater she wore.

Her gaze connected with his, and the light in her eyes dimmed.

Lynetta Spencer, the diner owner and Macey's aunt, rounded the counter with outstretched arms. She engulfed Macey in a tight hug. "Girl, it is so good to see you. When your mama said you were back home for good, I about fell off my stool."

"Hey, Aunt Lynetta. It's so great to see you." As Macey stepped out of her embrace, she shifted her eyes to Cole's, then muttered something to her aunt.

Lynetta raised an eyebrow and fisted a hand on her rounded hip as she seared him with a look. Then she headed to his table. An apron covered her full figure. Her dark hair, the same shade as Macey's, was twisted on top of her head in some sort of messy bun held in place by a yellow pencil.

Great. Would he need to find a new place to eat?

Lynetta cupped Lexi's cheek. "Hey, darlin'."

Lexi leaned into her touch, then held up her coloring book. "Hi, Miss Netta. Like my picture?"

Lynetta dropped on the bench next to her and slid an arm around his daughter's shoulders. "Sugar, that's the prettiest purple turtle I've ever seen."

Lexi tore it out and handed it to her. "Here, you can have it."

"Aww, thanks, precious. I'll hang it up behind the counter." She slid out from behind the table and stood. She pressed a gentle hand on Cole's shoulder, giving it a light squeeze. One eyebrow lifted, but her eyes softened. "I understand business, but that's my parents' property up for grabs. Your mom was like a sister to me, which makes you family too. I don't want to see anyone get hurt. Got it?"

Cole looked up at the woman who had been his mother's best friend since elementary school. The same woman who promised to look after Cole if anything should happen to her.

"Yes, ma'am. That wasn't my intention."

"My daddy's nice. He won't hurt nobody." Then Lexi's eyes lit up as she stood on the red vinyl bench and pointed. "Look, Daddy, there's Macey." She waved, her voice raising. "Hi, Macey."

All eyes in the diner turned to them, including Macey's. The reddened color of her face matched the round stools lining the counter. She smiled tightly and gave a little wave.

Lexi scrambled under the table and raced over to her, flinging her arms around Macey's legs. "Wanna sit with us?"

Without responding, Macey lifted Lexi in her arms and returned the hug. Then she set her down and took her hand, returning her to where Cole sat.

Lynetta eyed them. "Have you two kept in touch over the years?"

Cole scoffed. "Not exactly. Everly was offered a long-term subbing position at the elementary school, so Macey agreed to care for Lexi until I can find a more permanent solution."

Lynetta slid an arm around Macey's shoulder. "That's my girl. Always thinking of others. She's the best nanny a family could want."

"Lexi's been talking about her all afternoon, so I believe it."

Macey jerked her head toward the street. "Can I talk to you for a minute?"

Cole shifted his gaze to Lexi. Lynetta slid into the booth and picked up a crayon. "You two go. I'll keep an eye on this little one for a moment."

Cole hesitated. "If you're sure…"

Lynetta waved them way. "Go. Talk. The sooner you do, the better it'll be. For everyone."

He didn't know about that. But he followed Macey outside and stood on the sidewalk near the window so he could keep an eye on his daughter. He shoved his bare hands in his pockets to keep them warm. "What did you want to talk about?"

Macey rewrapped her scarf around her neck. "I want to know what you think you're doing."

He lifted a shoulder. "I'm planning to eat dinner with Lexi, my cousin Piper, and her daughter Avery."

Macey gave him an exasperated look. "I'm not talking about now. I'm talking about earlier in Fowler's office. What was that all about?"

Cole scrubbed a hand over his face. How many times were they going to rehash this? "We explained everything in Fowler's office. What else would you like to know?"

"Why my family's property? Why not property on the other side of town or even in a different area? Aspen Ridge isn't big enough for a strip mall."

"The property in question is near the highway and closest to Aspen Ridge. It makes more sense since it would bring more traffic into the community. Your family will be paid a fair market value."

"I'm so tired of hearing that phrase. You can't put a price on history. That section of the land was the original homestead when my great-great-grandparents settled the town. After Mom and Dad got married, my grandparents moved back to South Bend and restored the original house. Besides, all the traffic and noise from the strip mall will disturb the cattle. And Stone River cuts through our property. How will the construction affect the waterway? What about contaminants ruining the soil?"

"All of those issues will be addressed. We won't do anything to jeopardize the water supply, soil, or even the cattle. Besides, from the research I've done, it looks like your family could use the money."

Macey's eyes narrowed. "What does that mean?"

"Instead of talking to me, maybe you need to be talking to your family. There's more to this whole situation than you know. I understand wanting to protect family. I will do anything for my daughter. Crawford Developments will do everything to protect your family's property."

"If only I could believe you." She looked over his shoulder, a shadow filming her eyes.

Cole's fingers tightened into fists in his pockets. "Listen, Mace, I know you have trust issues when it comes to me, but I promise I didn't know about any of this when you agreed to care for Lexi. Talk to your family and see what they want to do. This wasn't my choice, but it's my job. Like you, I have plenty at stake as well."

"What? A promotion with a corner office view?"

Cole ground his jaw. "A promotion, yes. But a corner office means nothing to me. I care more about the medical benefits for my daughter." He paused a moment, then ran a hand over his face. "What does this mean for us? Caring for Lexi, I mean. And me helping you with the Sweetheart Ball."

Pocketing her hands, she sighed, white puffs of air punctuating her frustration. "I need the money and your little girl shouldn't suffer. Plus I don't have time to do all of the organizing on my own. But won't those be conflicts of interest for you now that you're overseeing this project?"

"I can separate business from my personal life." Even as he spoke the words, they didn't ring true to his own ears. Yeah, the next few months were going to be a challenge, but it wasn't anything he couldn't handle.

"But it's all personal. Don't you see that? I want what's best for my family and you want what's best for 'your daughter. Somehow, there needs to be a compromise." Without another word, she walked away.

The Macey Stone he knew growing up was more like the Macey who was so kind and patient with Lexi, not this angry person who was acting colder than the January air.

But could he really blame her? Honestly, he'd probably feel the same way.

Even though he'd said it wasn't personal, it was. For all of them. Somehow, he had to work it out for everyone's best interest.

Whatever that may be.

Chapter Three

If Macey couldn't get her family to join the fight with her, then why was she wasting her own time and energy? Somehow, they needed to come together as a united front.

Especially for Mom's sake.

Her mother sat in the same seat at the end of the rectangular dining room table for as long as Macey could remember. Her shoulder-length caramel-blond hair with streaks of gray around her temples had been pulled back into a clip, with a few wisps framing her face. Macey didn't like the deepening lines etching her mother's forehead, the brackets pinching her mouth, or the way she pushed her food around her plate.

Macey schooled her tone and tempered her anger as her gaze volleyed between her two brothers sitting across the table from her. "You guys don't get it. Saving the ranch needs to be our highest priority."

Bear threw his head back and laughed, the sound bouncing off the exposed beams. Raising his eyebrow, he pushed his empty plate away. His chair creaked as he leaned back and folded his arms over his chest. "*We* don't get it?" He wagged a finger between Wyatt and himself. "The two guys who have been working the ranch daily while you've been five hours away?"

She tried not to let his words get under her skin. Forcing a smile, she said to her brother, "I've been away doing my job."

He leaned forward, resting his arms on the table, and seared her with a glare. "Exactly. But you haven't been here on a daily basis, so you don't have any idea of what's happening. The least we can do is hear them out before rejecting their offer. Like Fowler said—they don't want the whole ranch. Just a portion of it."

"And a strip mall could help the town's economy." Wyatt wiped his daughter's face and handed her a plastic cup of milk.

"*Et tu*, Wyatt?"

Her younger brother held up his hands. "Hey, I'm not being a traitor. I'm simply looking at all sides."

"The letterhead may have the city council address, but now that we know they're using Crawford Developments, this has Wallace Crawford written all over it. He tried to buy South Bend once already, but Dad refused to sell. And for good reason. We need to keep what is ours."

"Ours? If you feel so strongly about the ranch, then why'd you run away the first chance you got?"

"I wouldn't exactly call going to college and getting a job running away." Macey wasn't about to rehash the past mortification that caused her to leave Aspen Ridge, but that didn't prevent the sting of her brother's words.

Macey's eyes darted between Mia, Wyatt's two-year-old daughter, and Tanner, her sister Mallory's five-year-old son sitting between Mom and Everly, who watched the grown-ups with wide eyes.

Mom cleared her throat. "Instead of arguing over dinner, we need to put it in God's hands and let Him work out the details."

Realizing she wasn't going to change her brother's mind, Macey swallowed her fighting words along with the last bite of her pot roast. She set her fork next to her plate and looked at him. "You're right, Bear. I haven't been around, but that doesn't mean I don't love the ranch or shouldn't know what's going on. Now that I'm home, I'll pull my weight around here and do what I can to help save the ranch."

"Even if saving it means letting go of a piece of it?" His tone gentled.

Was she willing to do that?

"Yes, even if saving it means letting go of a piece of it. I'm meeting with Cole soon, who's helping me with the Sweetheart Ball, so I'll get started on the dishes." She slid back her chair and carried her plate to the kitchen. She ran water in the sink and added a squirt of dish soap.

"We have a dishwasher, you know? No need to wash them by hand." Everly set her plate on the counter.

"I don't mind. Gives me time to think." Macey submerged her hands beneath the bubbles, allowing the heated water to warm her chilled fingers.

Standing behind Macey, Everly wrapped her arms around her sister's waist and pressed her cheek against Macey's back. "Thanks for helping me out with Lexi."

"You were right—she is a doll. We had fun baking cookies. Thanks for remembering about that. Otherwise, I would have had a very disappointed little girl on my hands. Are you ready for tomorrow?"

"As ready as I'll ever be, I guess. I'm sure it'll be a bit different than student teaching." Six years younger than Macey, Everly, with her lighter hair and blue eyes like their mom, looked more like a high schooler than an educator.

Mom carried in the plate of leftover pot roast and set it on the stove. She pressed her back against the counter and kneaded her temples.

"You okay, Mom?"

She lifted her head and gave them a tight smile. "Yes, just a little headache starting. I'll be fine."

"As soon as Macey and I finish the dishes, I'll drive you to the hospital so you can see Dad for a bit before bed." Everly turned to Macey. "You wanna go too, Mace? Dad'll be thrilled to see you."

Macey's hands stilled on the plate she was washing. "Thanks, but Cole's coming by to work on plans for the Sweetheart Ball with me. Give Dad my love though and let him know I'll come and visit soon."

Mom pushed away from the stove and reached for a dish towel. "Are you sure you have time to work on the ball, honey? I can cancel it or push it out further into the year, if need be."

As eager as she was to jump on that offer, the look on Mom's face had Macey swallowing her protest. Of course, she couldn't cancel. It wasn't that Macey didn't want to plan it. The thought of working with Cole still twisted her stomach in knots.

But she didn't want to burden her mother with stressing about her too.

Macey forced a smile into place. "Nope, it's not a problem, Mom. I've got it handled."

Mom slid an arm around her shoulders. "Thanks. I'm so glad I could count on you."

After cleaning the kitchen, Macey headed up the polished oak stairs to the room she'd shared with her sisters for the first eighteen years of her life and retrieved her laptop.

Family photos lined the tongue-and-groove paneled stairwell, showcasing the changes and additions to the family over the years, particularly the grandchildren.

With Mallory still in the navy and stationed on a carrier somewhere in the Pacific Ocean, her son Tanner lived at the ranch until her deployment ended in six months.

A knock sounded on the door. Macey hurried downstairs. She took a quick second to run a hand over her hair. Maybe she should've changed out of her jeans and sweatshirt she'd worn to help with barn chores before sitting down to dinner.

Knock it off.

She opened the door and cringed at the way Cole's presence sent her heart tripping over her ribs. "Cole. Hi, come in."

He stepped into the kitchen, stripped his black knit cap off his head, then smoothed down his hair.

Macey waved a hand to the table. "Have a seat. Want coffee or anything?"

He held up a hand as he pulled out a chair. "No, thanks. I'm good. I have only an hour or so before I have to pick up Lexi from Piper's."

"You could've brought her with you, you know."

"She wanted to hang out with Piper. Even though

they're second cousins, Piper's kind of like the only mother figure in Lexi's life right now."

"I remember Piper from school being very sweet and friendly to everyone. She and Bear used to be close until they had a falling out after her husband was killed."

"Ryland's death was tough all around."

"He was Bear's best friend. My brother hasn't been the same since that night. But you didn't come here to talk about the past." Macey lifted the cover of her laptop and opened the file her mother had sent with plans from previous years. "The ball's been held at the barn on South Bend for as long as I can remember. After my grandparents passed, my parents decided to continue the tradition." Then she stopped and glanced at Cole. "If this sale goes through, then this may be the last Sweetheart Ball on our family's property."

Cole shifted in his chair. "Then let's make the most of it to create a lasting memory."

"I don't want to create a lasting memory. I want to hold on to what's ours. But like Mom said over dinner— we need to put it in God's hands and let Him work out the details." Macey returned to the open document on her screen. "Aunt Lynetta and Uncle Pete will do the catering. I'm sure it will be a similar menu as in years past—an assortment of hors d'oeuvres, mixed green salad, a choice of filet mignon or roasted chicken, seasoned baby potatoes, vegetable medley and a dessert table. Tickets need to be purchased in advance to attend. They're on sale at the diner, and we'll sell them during WinterFest too. Mom said there was a problem with the posters, so they're being reprinted. Then they'll need to be hung up around town."

"Sounds like the bulk of the details are in place.

Other than hanging posters and selling tickets, what do we need to do?"

"Market the event, contact local businesses for prize donations, set up the barn at the homestead, decorate, show up and pray everything goes off without a hitch."

Cole grinned and snapped his fingers. "Piece of cake. You'll handle this like a pro. You're a natural organizer, which is why you were on the prom committee for three years in a row."

Macey held up a hand. "Can we not mention prom? Like ever again?"

"Sure, not a problem. Consider it stricken from my vocabulary."

Macey drummed her fingers on the table next to her laptop and bit her bottom lip. "How would you feel about me caring for Lexi here at the ranch? If I'm going to make the ball happen in less than a month, then I can't be tied to your condo all day. Plus she can play with Tanner and Mia here."

"As long as Lexi's in your very capable hands, I'm fine with you caring for her here. You're doing me a huge favor so I'll do whatever it takes to make things easier for you."

"Then stop the land sale from happening." The words tipped off the edge of her tongue before she had time to filter her thoughts.

"I really wish I could, Mace. The last thing I want is to bring you more pain."

She promised her family to listen to the offer and consider all sides. But was she truly willing to let it go even if that's what the family deemed was best?

Hopefully it wouldn't come to that.

Maybe having the Sweetheart Ball would show the

community the value of the property over having a strip mall that could endanger small businesses in town.

If Cole could find another suitable property like the parcel at Stone River Ranch, then maybe he could make his uncle happy and still salvage his relationship with the family who had been a huge part of his childhood.

Problem was, that strip of land *seemed* perfect for what Wallace wanted to build.

A strip mall could be an asset to the small ranching community, provided they attracted the right retailers.

But Cole really hated the idea of ruining the integrity of Aspen Ridge's small town feel by bringing in chain stores.

The town was straight out of a movie, which was why he'd stayed to raise his daughter after his ex-wife abandoned them.

Sure, a few chain restaurants would offer more variety, but they wouldn't have the same personal touch as Netta's Diner. However, Aspen Ridge's city council was serious about wanting to grow and offer sustainable jobs for the community. Would retailers even be willing to come to a town of less than four thousand residents?

Cole scrubbed a hand over his weary face.

After working on the ball with Macey, he'd spent the remainder of his Friday working past midnight. Then Wallace had called before six this morning, asking if Cole planned to work that day. Needing to keep his uncle happy, he agreed to half a day and asked Piper once again for help.

He'd dropped a teary-eyed Lexi off at his cousin's house at seven this morning and had been staring at the computer since seven thirty. He rubbed his burning eyes. With a sigh, he hit print, and the file of properties he compiled spit out from the printer.

He hadn't wanted to spend Saturday in the office, but if he could get his uncle to change his mind, then it would be worth the short time away from his daughter.

After pocketing his phone, he grabbed the pages and crossed the hall to Wallace's office.

His uncle, dressed in stiff Wranglers, a blue-and-white plaid pearl-snapped long-sleeved shirt and his worn cowboy boots, leaned back in his black leather executive chair and held the receiver of the office land-line to his ear.

Deep lines etched the man's weathered face, and his graying hair made him look like an Old West cowboy instead of the founder of a million-dollar corporation.

Cole rapped his knuckles against the open solid wood door. Wallace looked up and waved him in with two fingers.

Not wanting to eavesdrop on the call, Cole moved to the large window that offered a breathtaking snow-capped mountain view of the San Juan National Forest. With his office on the third floor of the building he owned, Wallace could look over Main Street to watch the daily activity of the business district. He liked to keep his finger on the pulse of what was happening in town.

The phone receiver rattled into its cradle and Wallace let out a whoop, causing Cole's heart to slam against his ribs. "Wylie's Western Wear just agreed to sit down with the council and discuss being one of the anchor stores in the strip mall. Great news, isn't it, son?"

He wasn't Wallace's son.

The man was nothing like Cole's father, who had

been killed on a job site when Cole was six, but he kept his mouth shut. After all, he still owed his uncle.

Cole clenched his jaw and turned, his fingers tightening on the sheaf of papers. "I was reviewing different properties around Aspen Ridge and surrounding communities. Maybe one of them would be a—"

"Why?" Wallace cut in, raising his right eyebrow—the man's tell for annoyance.

"Excuse me?"

"Why are you researching other properties? I want the Stone River Ranch property."

"I understand that, but one of these others would offer many of the same benefits and we wouldn't need to go after the Stones' land."

Wallace rounded his desk and walked toward Cole in slow, measured steps obviously meant to intimidate. Then he rested a heavy hand on Cole's shoulder, squeezing tighter than necessary. "Son, I don't pay you to second-guess me. If you're getting soft, I'll bring in someone who can close the deal. Is that what you want?"

Heat scorched Cole's neck, but he schooled his expression with a tight smile and shook off his uncle's hand. He lifted his chin and met the man's gaze. "No, sir."

Wallace grinned, reminding Cole again of a wolf watching his prey. "Good. Glad we understand each other. Now get with Fowler so the public notice can be posted. The quicker we act, the sooner we can be ready to break ground when the weather warms."

Wallace's phone buzzed. He moved to his desk and pressed the intercom. "What is it, Bernice?"

"Macey Stone is here to see you."

The man sighed. "Send her in."

Cole headed for the door, but Wallace blocked his path. "You might as well stay and hear what she has to say. Just be sure to tuck that bleeding heart away. Remember, this is business."

Macey appeared in the doorway, wearing jeans, and a white sweater under the red wool jacket she'd worn yesterday.

Wallace strode to the door with his hand outstretched. "Ms. Stone, come in and have a seat. What can I do for you?"

Macey ignored his hand and the invitation. Remaining in the doorway, she seared both of them with a fiery look. "You can stop the process of stealing my family's property."

Wallace laughed, but his eyes sparked. "Ms. Stone, you and I both know I'm not stealing anything. The city council is offering your family fair market value for a few acres. You will have plenty of land for your cattle. With your daddy laid up and Barrett licking his wounds over his fallen rodeo career, I hear the money will help keep your family's little ranch afloat a while longer."

"*Little* ranch? Our family has nearly a thousand acres."

"And my ranch in Montana has five thousand."

"Why are you doing this?"

He waved a hand toward Cole. "As I'm sure my property manager has explained, it's an opportunity to grow the economy. I'm merely working with the city council on this for the good people of Aspen Ridge."

"Right. You're telling me you have nothing to gain? You've always put yourself first and others second, Mr. Crawford. We'll fight you every step of the way."

"I'm sure you'll be a worthy adversary, young lady.

But just be sure you're doing what's best for your family. The longer this drags out, the less generous I... I mean, the city council may be."

"Is that a threat?"

"No threat. Simply stating I always get what I want."

"We'll see about that." She turned and strode out of Wallace's office, slamming the door behind her.

Wallace growled low in his throat, then reached for his Broncos coffee mug.

For a moment, Cole expected him to hurl it against the wall. Wouldn't be the first time.

Wallace drained the cup, then pierced Cole with a sharp look. "I don't care how you do it, but get them to sign. Otherwise, you'll find yourself out of a job. I'm sure you don't want that, especially with that expensive specialist your daughter needs that your insurance doesn't cover."

He flung the door open and marched down the hall, barking an order at Bernice.

Cole dragged a hand over his face, then returned to his office. He fed the lists of other properties through the shredder, feeling every bit sliced and diced as those bits of paper.

Somehow, he needed to show the Stones what a gain this could be instead of a loss.

Because Cole needed to keep this job for the sake of his daughter. Even if it meant working for a man like Wallace Crawford.

Chapter Four

Macey wasn't actually going behind her family's back. She simply wanted a second opinion.

But after the previous night's dinner conversation, she didn't expect them to be very receptive of her idea. She just didn't understand why they weren't as on fire to save the ranch. Especially after her impromptu meeting with the despicable Wallace Crawford.

How could Cole work for a man like that? Even if he was an uncle. What hold did that jerk have over him?

As Macey rounded the corner, her eyes drifted to the way the sun glazed the San Juan Mountains in the background of Main Street. Clouds crowned the peaks jutting against the brilliant blue sky. The aspens and frosted pines of the national forest and the silvery river flowing through the base eased the tightness in her chest.

There truly was no place like home.

"Hey, Macey. I heard you were back in town. Long time no see."

Macey whirled in the direction of the male voice and came face-to-face with Aaron Brewster, Allison's brother-in-law and one of her closest friends all through school. Just the person she'd come to see.

She hugged him and let out one of those little squeals she really disliked hearing from other people. "Aaron! It's so good to see you."

He wrapped his arms around her so tightly he lifted her off her feet. "I stopped by Cody and Allison's this morning, and Allison said you'd returned home. Why didn't you tell me you were coming?"

"It was a last-minute decision. Since I've been home, things have been busy."

Aaron's brows scrunched together behind his dark-rimmed glasses. Aaron wore faded jeans and a navy sweater beneath his yellow ski jacket. A light wind tugged at his short curly hair. "Everything okay?"

"Well, that's kind of why I'm here. I called your house, and Jacie said you were working this morning. Do you have a minute?"

Aaron looked at his watch. "I have about fifteen, then I have to meet a client."

"Honestly, I was a little surprised to learn you were open on a Saturday."

He shrugged. "I work until noon for those who can't come into the office during the week."

"Aaron Brewster—always caring for others. Mind if I just tell you quickly what I need?"

"What? And miss out on these billable minutes?" He laughed, a sound that Macey really missed. They'd had such good times together.

"Before I dive into my problem, how are Jacie and your little one doing?"

"Jacie's great." He nodded across the street. "She finally got the bridal shop up and running. Our little guy, Liam, turns two next month."

"I saw the storefront yesterday when I came into town. Between you and your brother, you're keeping your parents stocked with grandchildren."

"Cody and Allison have a head start on Jacie and me, but we're pretty happy." He glanced at his watch again. "So how can I help?"

"The ranch is in trouble."

He frowned. "How so?"

"The Aspen Ridge City Council sent my parents a letter of intent. They want to buy a portion of the ranch to create a strip mall. But I think Wallace Crawford is actually the brains behind this deal. And if we don't sell, they're claiming condemnation and going through the eminent domain process."

"Why does Aspen Ridge need a strip mall?"

"Exactly my question. My mom, Wyatt and I met with Mr. Fowler yesterday, but my impression was he was more for the council and Crawford than my family's interests, even though he's been our attorney since my grandparents were alive."

"What does your dad think about this?"

Macey shifted her feet and tightened her hold on her tote bag. "He doesn't know yet. Dad's in the hospital with possible pneumonia. Mom's waiting for more information before telling him."

"Not the homecoming you were hoping for, huh?"

"Not exactly. But that's a conversation for another day. I don't want to keep you from your appointment, but would you mind looking over the papers if I drop them off on Monday?"

"Not at all." Aaron pressed a quick kiss against her

cheek. "Great seeing you, Mace. Let's catch up when I have more time."

"Sure thing. Thanks. And give Jacie my love."

With a renewed sense of hope, Macey slid her bag onto her shoulder and headed across the street to the diner.

As she reached for the door, it swung open. She jumped back to avoid getting smacked in the forehead as a child raced out onto the sidewalk.

"Lexi, wait for me."

Macey recognized that deep voice.

Cole barreled through the open door and snagged Lexi around the waist.

"I was right here, Daddy. I wasn't going anywhere." Laughing, Lexi patted her chest.

"You are not allowed outside without me, and you know it. No arguments." He swung her in his arms.

"Sorry, Daddy." She rested her head on his shoulder.

He tightened his arms around her. "I forgive you, sweetheart. I just don't want anything to happen to my favorite Lexi."

"You're silly. I'm your only Lexi." The child's face lit up as she laughed. Lexi cupped her hands around Cole's clean-shaven face and rubbed her nose against his. Then her eyes connected with Macey's, and she waved. "Hi, Macey."

Cole turned, but his smile wasn't close to the sunshine his daughter exuded. He set Lexi down and held on to her hand.

Macey crouched in front of her. "Hey, Lexi. How's it going?"

"Netta made me sprinkle pancakes. Now Daddy's taking me to look at puppies. Wanna come?"

Macey snuck a glance at Cole. A muscle on the side of his jaw jumped as he lifted a shoulder. "I've never been a dog owner, so if you want to join us, I'd appreciate your input."

Macey turned her focus back to Lexi. "What kind of puppy are you going to get?"

Lexi lifted her hands and scrunched her face. "I don't know. Daddy says it needs to be little. Our 'partment is too small for Clifford the Big Red Dog." She cocked her head. "Does Clifford live at the shelter?"

Smiling, Macey shook her head. "I believe he still lives on Birdwell Island with Emily Elizabeth."

Lexi's eyes widened. "You know about Clifford?"

"Yep. My grandma used to read Clifford books to me when I was your age."

"I don't have a grandma."

Macey cupped the child's cheek and ran her thumb over the baby-soft skin. Then she shifted her attention to Cole. "Are you going to the shelter on Elk Avenue?"

"Yes, my mother worked there part-time when I was a kid, so I know Ray and Irene Douglas well."

"I remember. They're also my brother's in-laws. You may see Wyatt there. He helps them from time to time." Macey glanced at the diner, then looked back at Lexi. "I need to meet with Lynetta about the catering menu for the ball, but I can do that afterward. If you're sure... I don't want to intrude on your time with your daughter."

"It's all good." Cole pulled his keys out of his front pocket. "I'm parked across the street. You're welcome to join us." Then he touched her forearm as they headed for the crosswalk. "For what it's worth, I'm sorry for my uncle's attitude earlier. To him, this is just business."

"He'll destroy our family's legacy if this sale goes

through. A family that helped you when your mom became sick, remember?" The crosswalk light flashed green. Lexi skipped ahead with Cole only a few steps behind her.

Once they reached the sidewalk, Cole pressed a button on his key fob and unlocked his truck. He helped Lexi into her car seat, then held the door for Macey. As she passed him, his lips thinned. "I love your family very much, and you know it. The last thing I want is to hurt them. But I need this job and benefits for Lexi's sake. If this deal goes through, then he'll pay for treatments from one of the top pediatric audiologists in the state to help her. I'll always put my daughter's needs first. Even if it means making difficult business decisions relating to those I care about."

Macey pulled herself into the truck cab, then reached for the door. Despite her mounting frustration, she softened her tone. "He's a bully who's using you to do his dirty work. Surely there are other options. Can't you talk to him?"

Cole laughed, a hollow sound to Macey's ears, and shook his head. "I am one of the last people Wallace will listen to. He made that clear this morning when I tried to show him other properties just before you came in."

"Maybe you need to find a different job." Macey eyed Cole, noting the tender way his expression softened as he glanced back at Lexi.

"If only it were that simple." His words, a mix of sadness and resignation, slid out in a breathy whisper. He closed the door, rounded the front of the truck and slid into the driver's seat.

"Who's this specialist your uncle's dangling in front of you?"

"Some college buddy of Wallace's."

"So, he's purposefully withholding information until you do his bidding. So not fair. The man's a jerk." Macey softened her tone. None of this was Cole's fault, so she needed to back off and stop taking her frustrations out on him. "You're in a tough spot, Cole, and I'm sorry about that. I understand your need to do what's best for Lexi, but I need to do what's best for my family."

Bear's question from the other night echoed in her head. Despite her answer to him, would she be at peace if they had to give up the land she loved so much?

Hopefully, it wouldn't come to that.

No matter how much Cole wanted to convince Macey he truly had her family's best interests at heart, he had to put the land sale out of his mind and focus on his promise to look at puppies with Lexi.

When she'd invited Macey to join him, he wanted to veto the idea, but one look at Lexi's eager face had him swallowing his words.

Pulling into the parking lot of the Aspen Ridge Animal Shelter felt like coming home. Sitting on several acres at the end of Elk Avenue, the animal shelter was an extension of Ray and Irene Douglas's small farm. Their white sided two-story house with black shutters and a covered front porch sat to the left of the animal shelter, its front facing the driveway. A sidewalk connected the house to a large red barn edged against a grove of pines. Three blanketed horses stood in the fenced pasture near the barn.

The shelter building had been painted the same red as the barn, with the black trim matching the house.

Two leafless dwarf apple trees sat on either side of the building. A row of frosted shrubs lined the front. A plaster black Lab yard ornament holding a welcome sign sat next to a wrought-iron bench. The gravel semi-circle driveway had been blacktopped since his mother worked part-time as a kennel attendant.

Cole's mother always parked behind the building next to the other employees' vehicles, and they entered through the back door. Cole promised himself someday he'd park out front and go in the main door.

Today was that day.

Cole opened the passenger-side door, helped Macey down, then released Lexi from her car seat. Lexi took each of their hands as they walked through the door and were greeted by dogs barking and pawing at their glass-enclosed kennels.

Twirling in a circle, Lexi squealed and clapped her hands. "I'm so excited, Daddy."

He knelt in front of her. "I'm glad, but remember, we may not be able to take a doggy home today. We're just looking."

"I know. I'm still excited."

A woman with silver-streaked hair pulled back into a knot at the base of her head looked up. Wearing jeans, and a purple sweatshirt with the shelter logo in the upper left corner, she smiled as she rounded the corner of a chest high counter with her arms extended. Her eyebrow raised as she noticed Macey standing next to him. "Hey, Cole. It's so good to see you."

"Hey, Mrs. D. You look great." Walking into her embrace, he pressed a kiss against her soft cheek and breathed in the powdery scent he'd associated with her for so many years.

"Oh, you sweet talker, you." Then she reached for Macey. "Wyatt said you were back home. It's good to see you again, Macey. So, you two are together now?"

Macey threw up her hands and shook her head. "Oh, no. No, not at all. I'm caring for Lexi right now."

Cole sighed. Yeah, there was no way Macey would ever trust him enough to be friends, let alone anything more.

Mrs. Douglas crouched in front of Lexi. "How are you doing, Lexi?"

"I'm fine. Daddy said we could look at doggies today." Lexi leaned against Cole's legs and looked up at him.

Irene toyed with a curl that had escaped Lexi's ponytail, then trailed her finger down his daughter's cheek. She glanced up at Cole. "She looks so much like your mother. Janie would be so proud of you, you know?"

Nodding, Cole swallowed against the sudden tightness in his throat. "Mom would've loved her."

"Yes, she would have. I miss her. She was well loved and would do anything for anyone."

"That was my mom." An ache pinched his chest as he nodded again.

Mrs. Douglas straightened and clasped her hands in front of her, her eyes darting between Cole and Macey. "I tried to hire her away from the diner to work for me full-time, but Janie loved her customers. At least I got her in the afternoons for a couple of hours. My heart broke when she passed away."

Cole's vision started to cloud up and he blinked back tears. He hadn't expected this visit to be so emotional.

Yes, his mom would've been thrilled with Lexi. But

how would she have felt about Cole's role in trying to acquire the Stone land?

"So, do you have a particular breed you're interested in? Or a particular dog? Have you checked out our website? Filled out an application?" Mrs. Douglas waved a hand toward the glass-walled kennels that allowed visitors to see dogs napping on their beds, chewing on toys, or pawing to be freed.

"No, I guess I didn't come very prepared." Cole glanced at Macey who knelt in front of the glass-walled kennels where a fluffy black-and-white dog lay on a dog cot and watched them.

Mrs. D. dismissed his words with a wave of her hand. "No worries. Right now, we have six dogs ready for their forever homes. If you give me an idea of what you're looking for, then I can help you find the right match."

"We're living in a condo until I can find the right house with a good-sized yard, so the dog needs to be small, calm and definitely kid friendly."

Mrs. Douglas steepled her fingers, touching them to her chin, then smiled. "I think I have just the dog for you, but she won't be ready for adoption for another week. Follow me."

Cole gestured for Macey to walk ahead of him, then set his hand at the small of her back as she stayed in line with him. They passed the enclosed kennels as memories flooded him.

While his mother had worked, Cole loved sitting in the play yard with the dogs tumbling over him. They didn't care what kind of clothes he wore or the brand of shoes on his feet. They just wanted love and attention... and a place to call home. He would've been a great dog owner. But no matter how many times he had pleaded, his mother never gave in to his request for an animal.

Looking back now, they couldn't have afforded it. Despite all of her efforts and the two jobs she held, they'd barely had enough to support the two of them.

Mrs. Douglas guided them to an office across the hall from the kennels. "Have a seat in here, and I'll bring Polly to see you."

Macey sat on a brown microfiber love seat. Because it was the only seat in the office, Cole sat next to her, his shoulder brushing against hers. He hugged the arm to give her more room and pulled Lexi onto his lap. A calico cat walked into the room and rubbed its head on Cole's legs.

Lexi gasped. "Look, Daddy. It's a kitty."

She jumped off his lap and wrapped her arms around the cat.

Macey scooted off the love seat and sat next to her. "Lexi, you have to be careful. You don't know if that kitty likes hugs."

At that moment Mrs. Douglas entered the room holding a purple leash connected to a small black-and-white dog with wavy hair. "Not to worry. Hawthorne loves everyone."

She brought the dog closer to them. Its little nose sniffed Lexi. "And this cutie is Polly. She's a schnoodle."

"Schnoodle? What's that?" Cole leaned forward and ran his fingers over Hawthorne's fur.

"A miniature poodle and a miniature schnauzer mix. She was surrendered to us recently when her owner moved into assisted living and could no longer care for her. Polly is about six years old, apartment friendly and she loves small children. Her previous owner had a large family with several small grandchildren. Unfortunately, none of them were able to take the sweet girl. She's been with us for a couple of weeks, and our vet hasn't released her for adoption just yet. But she will be ready in a week for a new home."

Hawthorne left Cole and wound his way around Mrs. Douglas's legs. Still holding on to Polly's leash, she scooped up the cat and placed him on the tower in the corner.

Cole moved to the floor next to Lexi and waited for the dog to approach them again. "Hey, Polly. How are you doing?"

The dog's ears perked, and she cocked her head at the sound of her name.

Mrs. Douglas opened a container on the desk in the corner and grabbed a handful of tiny dog treats. She gave a few to Macey, then handed the rest to Cole. "See if she'll take these treats, one at a time, out of your hand."

Cole placed a treat on his palm. Polly took a few tentative steps, licked her lips and took the treat.

Mrs. Douglas crouched and petted the dog's head. "Good girl, Polly." She looked at Lexi. "Would you like to try feeding her?"

Eyes wide, Lexi nodded. Then she looked at Cole. "Can I, Daddy?"

"Sure. Just do what I did. Put the treat in your hand and hold it flat for Polly to take."

Lexi did as instructed, then giggled as Polly ate the treat. Lexi rubbed her hand on her shirt. "Her tongue tickles."

"Yes, it does."

They played with Polly for another fifteen minutes, allowing Lexi and Polly to get used to each other.

"I think we've found a match." Cole pulled his phone out of his pocket and snapped a picture of his daughter petting Polly. "What's the next step?"

"We'll fill out some paperwork. Usually, we suggest a trial stay to make sure the dog is the right fit for your family. Then, you can decide if you'd like to make her a permanent addition to your household."

"What do you think, honey?"

Lexi petted the dog curled in her lap. "Polly needs us, Daddy."

His daughter's tender heart never ceased to amaze him. He pushed to his feet. "Okay, then. Let's fill out some paperwork. The week we wait for her to be released will give me time to get food and supplies for her."

"Sounds good."

Cole turned to Macey. "Would you mind staying here with Lexi and Polly while I fill out the paperwork?"

Smiling, Macey ran a hand over Polly's fur. "Not at all. We're good here."

"Thanks." He knelt in front of Lexi. "Hey, squirt, stay here with Macey and I'll be right back. I need to sign papers so Polly can come live with us."

"Okay, Daddy." She didn't take her eyes or hands off the dog in her lap.

As he followed Irene back to the front counter, the back door opened.

Wyatt Stone walked in, carrying a large bag of dog food. "Hey, Mama D. I stopped by the feed store, and Drake donated another bag of food."

"Thanks, hon. Put it in the prep room, and I'll call Drake later and thank him."

Wyatt disappeared around the corner, then returned a moment later. He crossed the room, hand extended. "Hey, Cole. How you doing, man?"

Cole hesitated a moment, a little surprised by Wyatt's pleasant attitude. He shifted away from the counter and shook his hand. "Good. And you?"

"Can't complain." Wyatt glanced around. "No Lexi?"

Cole jerked his head toward the office. "Actually, she's in the other room with Macey and our new schnoodle, Polly."

"Macey, huh?" Wyatt grinned.

Shrugging, Cole ignored his friend's implication. "Lexi invited her."

"And no one can say no to Lexi, am I right?"

"One of my greatest struggles."

Wyatt gave him an understanding nod. "Oh, I hear you. I'm there myself with Mia. Thank God for my family. Hey, listen—I gotta get back to the ranch, but the offer to join my single fathers support group is still open. Or give me a call any time with questions or concerns. I don't have all the answers, but the group has men from all walks of life. They've been a great support system."

"Thanks, I appreciate it." Cole looked over his shoulder as Macey and Lexi walked hand in hand into the reception area with Lexi holding Polly's leash. "We're doing fine, just the two of us."

But even as he spoke, his words sounded hollow. His daughter needed more than what he could offer. She needed a woman's touch.

Someone like Macey.

But that wasn't going to happen. Especially with this land sale building a wall between them.

Wyatt crouched and petted Polly. "Hey, Polly. Looks like you found a new home."

Lexi's eyes widened as she knelt beside him. "You know Polly?"

"Sure. Polly and I became buddies after I took her for a couple of walks." Wyatt straightened, then glanced between Macey and Cole. "Why don't you stop out at the ranch? I'm sure Lexi would enjoy seeing the horses."

"Horses? Really?" Lexi scrambled to her feet, nearly rolling Polly onto the floor. "Can I ride one, Daddy?"

Cole shot Wyatt a "Thanks, pal" look, then turned back to his daughter. "I don't know, Lexi."

"Why not?" She pointed to Wyatt. "That man said I could. I heard him."

"I believe he said you could see them." Cole's gaze shifted between Wyatt and Macey, whose tight smile signaled she was less than impressed with her brother's suggestion. "Wouldn't it be a conflict of interest, considering I'm working for my uncle?"

Wyatt lifted a shoulder. "Doesn't have to be. You grew up with us, man. You've been to the ranch more times than I can remember. You've been like family before you ever worked with your uncle."

And that was a part of the problem.

Lexi dropped Polly's leash and grabbed his leg. "Please, Daddy?"

"What do you think, Mace?"

She lifted a shoulder. "Wyatt invited you. This is between you guys."

Staring down at Lexi's big blue eyes, Cole felt his resolve slipping. He gripped the back of his neck. "Okay, fine."

Even though Lexi clapped and danced with Polly spinning in circles next to her, Cole didn't share her enthusiasm.

In fact, his clenched gut said it was a very bad idea.

But how could he say no to his daughter?

Chapter Five

Macey needed just an hour or so by herself.

Time to think and come up with some way to combat Crawford's attempt to gain access to their land.

Once word had spread about the council's desire for the strip mall, many of their friends and neighbors had expressed their outrage and promised to stand with the Stones.

But was it enough?

Because for all who wanted to protect their property, an equal number—or more—were in favor of the strip mall.

Even a week later, Bear still remained a little cool toward her. Macey kept her mouth shut because she didn't want to add to Mom's growing fatigue.

Before her mother left for the hospital this morning, Macey suggested taking her place so she could rest, but Mom had said if she stopped, she was afraid she'd fall apart. She needed to be strong now and could rest later.

But what was that strength costing her? Costing all of them?

So Macey spent the last week doing what she could

to help ease her burdens at home, like doing Mom's barn chores, housecleaning and getting dinner on the table. Although sitting at the dining room table still didn't feel right without Dad at the head.

Now she wanted a quick ride before returning to the ranch house to make lunch for everyone.

Since coming back from Denver, she'd been surrounded by people. And she loved it, especially being with her mom again.

When she wasn't caring for Lexi, helping on the ranch, or working on the plans for the ball, she lent a hand at the diner and chatted with customers, getting their views about the proposed strip mall.

A quick getaway by herself would refresh her enough to face the upcoming week.

Morning sunshine warmed her face as she headed to the barn. With temperatures above freezing and the sun shining over melted snow, today seemed like the perfect day to ride and clear her head.

Her worn cowboy boots hugged her feet like old friends, and the hat she dug out of her closet took her back to riding South Bend with Grandpa. Maybe that sudden feeling of nostalgia was why she was so intent on heading out to her grandparents' property. Especially if Crawford got his way and took over the land.

She entered the barn, allowing a few seconds for her eyes to adjust to the changes in light. After breathing in the sweet scent of hay and the rich scent of saddle leather, she exhaled slowly, forcing her shoulders to relax.

Heading to Cheyenne's stall, she slid the door open and stepped inside.

Her quarter horse lifted her head and eyed Macey.

"Hey, Chey. Wanna go for a ride?" She ran a hand over the mare's gleaming chestnut coat and rested her cheek against Cheyenne's neck. Taking the mare by the halter, she led her into the aisle. She cross-tied her by clipping the lead straps to both sides of Cheyenne's halter for her protection as well as Macey's.

After taking the hoof pick out of the grooming basket, Macey moved to Cheyenne's side and ran her hand down the mare's leg. Cheyenne lifted her foot.

Macey removed a couple of small stones from the horse's hoof, then repeated the same process for the other three hooves.

She exchanged the hoof pick for a brush. With a hand on the horse's hip, Macey talked to her in soothing tones as she removed bits of hay and debris from Cheyenne's coat.

Macey tossed the brush into the basket and headed to the tack room. She draped the reins over her arm and lifted her saddle off the rack. She grabbed a pad and carried everything back to the aisle where the horse stood patiently.

Macey set everything on the bench across from Chey's stall. She reached for the saddle pad, settling it on the horse's withers.

A childish giggle followed by low-toned male voices outside the barn caused Cheyenne's ears to twitch. The barn door opened, sweeping in chilly air, and shadows spilled across the floor. Wyatt, Cole and Lexi headed inside.

Even though Wyatt had invited Cole and Lexi to come and see the horses last week while they talked at the animal shelter, Macey was still surprised he'd actually shown up at the ranch.

So much for her quiet retreat to South Bend.

"Hey, Mace. Whatcha doin'?"

She straightened the saddle pad and lifted her head. Wyatt and Cole stood in front of Cheyenne's stall. Wyatt's arms rested on the door as he grinned like an annoying little brother. Macey glanced at him, then lifted an eyebrow at Cole, who wore a buckskin-colored cowboy hat with a black band that shadowed his face.

She forced a casual tone in her voice. "You came."

Before Cole could speak, Wyatt pushed away from the stall and folded his arms over his chest, feet shifting apart, every bit the former marine. "I invited him here, remember? So be nice, sis."

"I'm always nice." She eyed Cole, daring him to challenge her words, then swiveled her attention back to her brother. "What are you guys doing?"

"We're going to take Lexi for a ride." He lifted a chin at Cheyenne. "You riding too?"

Macey lifted the saddle onto Chey's back. "I planned to ride to South Bend and shoot some photos of the waterfalls."

"Glad to hear you're getting back into your photography. Mind if we tag along?"

Macey cocked her head and lowered her voice. "Seriously, Wy?"

He lifted a shoulder and glanced at Cole. "Sure, why not?"

Macey swallowed a sigh. "Don't you think it's a conflict of interest?"

Wyatt shook his head and shoved his hands in his back pockets. "I see it as old friends taking a ride together."

"Apparently, my vision's a bit cloudier than yours."

She turned back to the mare and cinched the saddle in place. "Suit yourself. I can't tell you what to do."

"Great. You lead, and we'll follow. That way, you can get the shots you want and I can help Cole with Lexi."

Seeing Cole in worn jeans with a threadbare, navy pullover hoodie that stretched across his chest messed with Macey's concentration. Not to mention the morning scruff on his unshaven chin. Why did he have to look so good, no matter what he wore? Then, he settled his hat back on his head, shadowing his face once more.

Macey's heart thunked against her rib cage. She needed to leave the barn before she did or said something stupid.

Lexi ran up to her and wrapped her arms around Macey's jean-clad legs. "Hi, Macey. I'm so excited to ride a horsey today."

Looping the reins around her wrist, Macey leaned over and hugged the child, who was dressed in jeans with embroidered butterflies on the thigh and a pink hooded puffy coat. An oversize pink cowboy hat sat on her hair, which framed her face in two lopsided braids. "Hey, sweet girl. It's so good to see you. I like your hat."

Lexi patted its crown. "My Piper let me borrow it. She said cowgirls needs hats. Do you know her?"

Macey nodded as she put herself between the child and Cheyenne's muscular legs. Not that the gentle horse would kick, but with Lexi's sudden movements, it was better to err on the side of caution. "I know your Piper. She's friends with my sisters."

Cole scooped up his daughter. "Lexi, let's leave Macey alone, okay?"

"She's never a bother." Macey's eyes connected with Cole's.

His eyebrow arched as if to ask if he was the one who bothered her.

Needing space between them, Macey closed the stall door, snatched her camera bag off the post, then led Cheyenne out of the barn.

She squinted against the morning sunshine and lowered the brim of her hat to shield her eyes. Holding on to the saddle horn, she put her left foot in the stirrup and threw her right leg over the horse. The leather squeaked as she settled in her seat. She gathered the reins and gave Cheyenne a gentle nudge with her knee and clicked her tongue. "Come on, girl. Let's get out of the way so these guys can saddle up."

She lifted her face and breathed deeply, allowing the sun's rays to warm her skin against the cool air that cleared her lungs. Guiding Cheyenne toward the gravel road that led away from the ranch, she glanced over her shoulder to find the doorway to the barn empty.

Maybe she could snag a few moments of quiet before they joined her.

As Cheyenne trotted through the open Stone River Ranch gate, Macey glanced over her shoulder once again. This time, Wyatt rode Dante, his black stallion, while Cole followed on Patience, Mom's mare, with Lexi seated in front of him.

A gentle breeze whisked over her heated cheeks as she guided Cheyenne down the dirt road toward South Bend.

"Go faster, Daddy!" Lexi's giggles competed with Patience's hooves thundering against the road, kicking up melting snow and mud.

The man seemed quite comfortable in a saddle.

Macey pulled up on Cheyenne's reins and tied them

loosely around the saddle horn. She removed her camera from her bag and attached the lens, manually focusing the men in her viewfinder. After snapping a few pictures, she zoomed in on the joy lighting up Lexi's darling face.

Then Macey dismounted and snapped a few shots of Cheyenne against the backdrop of the San Juan Mountains.

"Whoa." Wyatt pulled on Dante's reins and brought his black stallion to a stop next to Macey. Cole flanked the other side of her.

"Look, Macey, I'm riding a horsey." Lexi pulled off her hat and waved it, her cheeks pink from the weather and the excitement.

Macey grinned and lifted her camera one more time. "You sure are, sweetheart. Are you having fun?"

The child nodded and leaned back against Cole. "Daddy said I can take lessons when I turn five." She held up a splayed hand. "Someday I can ride all by myself. He said until then I have to ride with him to stay safe."

"Yes, it's so important to stay safe. I learned how to ride with my daddy too. Just like you're doing." Macey framed Lexi and caught Cole's profile as he leaned down and kissed the top of his daughter's head.

Dismounting, Wyatt nodded toward the path that cut through the trees. "Let's take the trail to the homestead." His eyes volleyed between Macey and Cole, then he nodded to Lexi. "Cole, want to ride Dante? Lexi can stay on Patience, and I'll walk the horse."

A look of apprehension flashed across Cole's face, but at Lexi's high-pitched squeal, he replaced it with a laugh. "I guess we have Lexi's answer."

Wyatt held on to Lexi while Cole dismounted. After instructing Lexi how to hold on to the saddle horn, Wyatt picked up Patience's reins. He led them slowly down the rutted trail through the grove of pines frosted with snow.

Cole put his leg in Dante's stirrup and lifted his other leg over the stallion's back.

Macey mounted Cheyenne again and pulled up next to him. "No Saturday meeting today?"

"Only if the boss wants one."

"Doesn't he care about what you want?"

He lifted a shoulder. "What I want isn't relevant. At least not right now. My number one concern is ensuring Lexi has the best care possible. And if that means appeasing my uncle for now, then I'll meet with him on a Saturday. It's only for an hour or so anyway."

"Care for what? If you don't mind me asking. After you mentioned her medical condition, I did a little research. There's a lot to neurofibromatosis."

"Yes, there is. And each case is different. As I mentioned last week—Lexi's hearing is being affected, and she needs hearing aids. We meet with the pediatric audiologist next month. I have to keep a close eye on her because when she gets sick, it hits her hard and she usually ends up in the hospital. I try to keep her as healthy as possible to avoid that. Plus Wallace isn't as accommodating as he could be when it comes to dealing with Lexi's medical history."

"Why not find another job?"

Cole let out a sigh as his gaze drifted across the pasture. "I owe him."

"What do you mean?"

"After Mom died, Wallace took care of me and paid for my education. In exchange, I work for him."

"Sounds like he's taking advantage of the situation."

"It is what it is. This promotion promises even more money and better benefits for Lexi, so I'm letting him pull my strings."

"That's why you're pushing for my family to sign."

"It's only a portion of the property."

"Maybe so, but it's still our property. My parents shouldn't be bullied into selling. I do see your dilemma, though. What happens if your uncle doesn't get the land for some reason? For you and Lexi, I mean."

Cole lifted his hat and scratched the back of his head. Then he set it back in place. "I don't know. And honestly, I really don't want to find out."

"I'm sorry you have to go through this alone with very little family support. I'm sure you know this already, but there are programs in place to help children like Lexi get the quality care she needs. Then you wouldn't have to rely on this job so much."

"My mother taught me we take care of our own. We don't accept handouts. Call it family pride or whatever, but as long as I can provide the care Lexi needs, then that leaves room in those programs for families who can't afford them any other way. Listen, Mace. I don't expect you to understand. The last thing I want is to cause your family any pain, but I truly have to put my daughter's needs first."

Even at the cost of her family's future.

Wyatt whistled, jerking Macey's attention to the end of the trail where her brother had stopped leading Patience. He turned the horse and led her back to Cole and Macey. His eyes darkened, and lines bracketed his tight mouth.

"What's going on, Wyatt?" Cole dismounted.

"Macey, take everybody back to the ranch, then send Bear out here. We've got trouble."

Dante nickered as if sensing his owner's stress and danced in place. Wyatt pressed a hand against the stallion's neck.

"What kind of trouble?"

"There's a crew on ranch property without our permission. And I'm going to find out what they're doing there." Then his gaze skated to Cole. "It may be a good idea for them not to see you."

Nodding, Cole's jaw tightened as his eyes darted between the trail opening and his daughter.

Even if Macey didn't agree with Cole's choices, the last thing she wanted was for him to lose his job, particularly now that she knew more of his motivations.

But should her family give up without a fight? There was no easy win in this situation.

Wallace's harsh accusations blistered Cole's ears as he ducked his head against the sleet and headed for his truck.

A call from Macey about Lexi not feeling well had him leaving work, which didn't score points with his uncle who was still furious with him.

As he headed back to his condo, he replayed his recent conversation with his uncle. Could he have handled it differently?

Once Wallace had appeared on the job site on Monday morning following Cole's visit to the ranch, Cole questioned him about the Crawford Developments crew being on Stone River property without permission.

Well, that blew up in Cole's face because his uncle accused him of spying and working with the enemy.

How could he get his uncle to see the Stones weren't the enemy? The man was blinded by his hatred of Deacon Stone and driven to acquire the property by whatever means possible.

Somehow Cole needed to put that conversation out of his head and refocus his attention on his daughter.

Which was one more reason for his uncle to blast him for leaving to care for her.

The man didn't have an ounce of compassion in his narcissistic body.

But Cole didn't care. Lexi had to come first, and if Wallace wanted to fire him...well, it sure would solve a lot of problems.

Except the medical insurance issue.

Even then, he'd make that work.

Somehow.

Macey was right—there were programs in place to help Lexi. Every time Cole started to check them out, though, his mother's words and that long-ago argument resurfaced.

We do not accept charity, Cole Edward Crawford. We will make our own way in the world.

Too bad his mother's way meant working herself to death at a way too young of an age, leaving Cole at his uncle's mercy despite his begging to stay with Lynetta and Pete Spencer. The court deemed a blood relative was more important than one of the heart.

The only brother of Cole's father, Wallace provided everything Cole needed materially. He'd finished his high school years wearing name brand clothes and driving a car that didn't break down every fifty miles. Then he'd paid for Cole's college tuition with the understanding Cole would work for his uncle after graduation and pay him back for what he'd done for him.

A price that cost Cole a lot more than he'd ever expected.

While he tried to be grateful because Wallace had pulled him out of poverty, the man had a heart the size and hardness of a marble.

Gruff may work in the boardroom or on the job site, but not where Lexi was concerned. Especially when she was sick.

Sleet bulleted Cole's windshield as he parked in front of the condo and hurried through the storm to his front door.

He entered the code and stepped inside. Polly barked, jumped off the couch and raced to him.

After their trail ride over the weekend, Mrs. Douglas had called to say Polly had been released by their vet for adoption.

Still excited from riding a horse, Lexi had been over the moon when he shared the news and begged to pick up Polly that evening.

Even though the little dog had been with them only a couple of days, she seemed to be settling in well.

Kicking off his wet shoes, he scooped her up and hurried into the living room where Lexi lay on her side with her knees pulled to her chest. Dried tear trails streaked her face as her eyes remained closed.

He set Polly on the floor then knelt on one knee and brushed back the hair falling out of her ponytail. "Hey, Lexi Lou. Daddy's here."

With eyes still closed, she smiled and whispered, "I'm not Lexi Lou, I'm Lexi Jane."

"Cole."

Cole looked up and saw Macey standing in the kitchen doorway, holding a dish towel. "Hey, Mace. What's going on?"

"Lexi didn't want to eat her snack this morning. When I touched her forehead, she felt warm, so I took her temp. It was 100.2, and she's complaining that her right ear is hurting. I brought her back here so she could rest in her own space. That's when I called you."

"I'm glad you did. Thanks for that, by the way. She seemed fine this morning when I dropped her off at the ranch. A little sleepy, but I didn't think too much of it." Guilt gnawed at him as he cupped his daughter's warm cheek. "Have you given her Tylenol or anything?"

A tender look in her eyes, Macey shook her head. "I wanted to wait and see what you'd like to do."

"I'll call her pediatrician and see if I can get Lexi an appointment today."

"Daddy, my ear hurts." Tears leaked out of her tired-looking eyes.

"Show me which one."

She covered her right ear with her small hand.

He kissed her forehead and felt the heat radiating off her skin. "I'll call Dr. Jeanette and see if she can look in your ears today, okay?"

Lexi nodded and rested her head against Cole's hand.

He reached for his phone and hit the pediatrician's office number on his speed dial. When the receptionist answered, he explained the situation and swallowed a sigh of relief when she mentioned a last-minute cancellation. If he could be there in ten minutes, then the pediatrician could see her right away.

Cole relayed the information to Macey. "You can head home, if you want."

"You sure? You won't need to return to work? You paid me for the full day."

"I'll let Wallace know Lexi's sick, and that I'll work from home for the rest of the day."

"Okay. I'm going to swing by the diner and talk to Lynetta about the ball. Let me know if anything changes and you need me to come back."

"Thanks, I will."

Forty minutes later, Cole dashed through the sleet, careful not to slip on the icy blacktopped driveway, and buckled Lexi in her car seat. They'd sat in the busy waiting room for nearly thirty minutes, then saw the pediatrician for ten. Now, Lexi's chest shuddered from spent tears after getting her inflamed ears checked.

Double ear infection. And her temperature had risen to 102 degrees. Thankfully, the prescription for an antibiotic had been called in to the pharmacy already.

Cole turned on Lexi's favorite radio station and pulled out of the parking lot. As he headed to the pharmacy, Lexi spoke up from the back seat. "Daddy, I want pancakes."

"Okay, punkin. I'll make you some as soon as we get back home."

"Nooo, Daddy," she wailed, turning her head and crying into her hood. "I want Netta's pancakes."

Normally, Cole did not give in to temper tantrums, but his heart melted at his daughter's sobs. If pancakes would help her to feel better, then he'd do what he could to help. He tapped the voice command on his steering wheel. At the prompt, he said, "Call Netta's Diner."

The phone rang on the speakerphone. "Netta's Diner, how may I help you?"

The voice sounded similar to the diner owner's, but with Lexi's crying in the back seat, he couldn't quite tell for sure. "Lynetta?"

"No, this is Macey. Lynetta's not available."

"Macey, it's Cole. Hey, I need to place a take-out order of pancakes for Lexi."

"Sure, Cole. Anything else?"

"No, just the pancakes. Lynetta knows how she likes them."

"Lynetta stepped out for a few minutes. I'm minding the register until she gets back."

Cole bit back a groan and glanced in the rearview mirror to see if his daughter had been paying attention to the conversation. "Okay, I'll just take them however they come. I need to swing through the pharmacy drive-through, then I'll be by to pick them up. When I get there, is there any way someone could run them out to me? Lexi has a double ear infection, and I really don't want to take her inside if I don't have to."

"Take her home, and I'll bring the pancakes to you."

"You don't have to do that."

"I planned to return anyway so you could go back to work. Just get Lexi home so she can feel better."

He turned into the pharmacy drive-through lane. "Great. Thanks. You have no idea how much I appreciate it."

"Aunt Lynetta would do the same."

Less than ten minutes later, Cole carried a sleeping

Lexi back inside. Polly greeted them at the door again with a bark and a dance to welcome them home.

Ignoring the little dog for a moment, he changed Lexi out of the polka-dot leggings and long-sleeved light purple T-shirt he'd helped her put on that morning and back into the unicorn pajamas she'd tossed on her bed. He got her settled under her favorite mermaid blanket on the couch and turned on the soft classical music station she liked to help her stay asleep. Polly jumped on the couch and licked Lexi's cheek.

Her face scrunched as she pushed the dog away.

Cole scooped up the fur ball, cradled her to his chest, then set Polly on the other end of the couch. This time, she curled against the curve of Lexi's legs bent at the knee.

A quiet knock sounded on the front door, sending Polly off the couch and barking at the door.

He hurried across the room, scooped up the dog again and opened the door. Macey stepped inside, clutching a large take-out bag.

He took the bag from her, set it on the side table inside the door, then reached for his wallet. "What do I owe you?"

Cheeks pink, Macey bit down on her mitten and pulled it off. She waved her hand, dismissing his question. "It's been taken care of."

Cole scowled. "What do you mean?"

"When Aunt Lynetta came back, she made Lexi's pancakes and insisted on adding eggs and juice. Plus a burger and fries for you. Then she said it was on the house."

Cole pulled out a twenty and held it out to Macey.

"I appreciate her thoughtfulness, but I can pay my own way."

Macey folded her hand over his, crushing the money between his fingers and palm. "No one said you couldn't. But when someone else wants to do something nice for you, just say thank you.

"Thank you." Heat warmed Cole's neck. "You don't need to stay. I can spend the rest of the afternoon working here."

Macey shifted her feet and looked at him hesitantly. "Aunt Lynetta asked me to check on Lexi and report back to her. So if you don't mind me taking a quick peek…"

"Well, I wouldn't want to get you in trouble with the boss." Grinning, Cole closed the door behind her. He nearly bumped into Macey as he turned around. Her hair brushed against his chin, releasing the floral scent of her shampoo.

He grabbed her arms as her hands flew to his shoulders. His eyes locked with hers as he loosened his hold. "Whoa. Sorry about that. I didn't expect you to be so close."

He certainly didn't mind, though.

Being around Macey almost daily for the past couple of weeks reignited feelings he'd thought long gone.

But they were friends, and that was all they ever could be.

With everything else on his plate, the last thing he needed was to fall for the daughter of his uncle's enemy.

No matter how well she cared for his child and fit into their lives.

Chapter Six

Macey should've gone back to the ranch instead of stopping at the diner.

Then she wouldn't have been there when Cole called. And she wouldn't have ended back up at his place. Or nearly in his arms.

Stepping back, she dropped her fingers as if his shoulders had been on fire and shook her hands. "No, it's my fault. I didn't move in far enough."

Trying to distract herself from the lingering feel of Cole's strong hands on her shoulders, Macey picked up Polly and rubbed her cheek over the dog's soft fur. "Polly seems to be settling in well."

"It's been only a couple of days, but she and Lexi adore each other. I hope it wasn't too chaotic this morning with her and Lexi not feeling well." He grabbed the bag and carried it into the kitchen, the scent of grilled meat wafting between them. "Can I get you anything to drink? Coffee? Water? Juice box?"

"I'm good. And no, it wasn't a problem. Polly is a sweetie." Smiling, she held up a hand as she moved silently toward the couch. She returned Polly to her spot behind Lexi's legs. Leaning over Lexi's sleeping form, she ran a finger over the little girl's cheek, feeling the elevated warmth. "Poor thing."

Macey straightened and headed for the kitchen.

Cole removed the cardboard to-go boxes and flipped up the lid. The hot scent of salted fries hit her. To her horror, her stomach growled.

Smirking, Cole nudged the overflowing box toward her. "Maybe you need this more than I do."

"Actually, I had a salad before lending Aunt Lynetta a hand."

He opened the cabinet above the microwave and pulled down a couple of plates. "Want to split the burger?"

Leaning against the counter with one arm pressed against her traitorous stomach, Macey shook her head but snitched a fry. "No, thanks, but I wouldn't say no to a fry or two."

"Take as many as you'd like. I don't need to eat all of them." Ignoring the plate, he reached for the burger and stood over the sink, biting into the juicy sandwich. "Man, that tastes good. I'd eat at the diner for all my meals if my wallet could afford it."

"While I love Aunt Lynetta and Uncle Pete's food, I don't think my waistline could handle it on a daily basis."

Cole raised an eyebrow. "Like you have anything to worry about."

She dipped her head, but not before heat crawled across her face.

Cole devoured the burger, then wiped his fingers on a paper napkin snatched from the take-out bag. "Guess I was hungrier than I thought." He peered into the liv-

ing room. "Apparently, Lex needs sleep more than pancakes right now. I really need to get Lynetta's recipe so
I don't have to bother you guys every time she wants
pancakes. Which would be daily if she had her way.
Thank you again for delivering them."

"It wasn't a bother. Really. I was heading back to
the ranch, so this was on my way." Macey glanced at
the sleeping child, then refocused on Cole. "She's very
special. But I don't have to tell you that, do I?"

Cole's eyes drifted to his daughter and he shook his
head. "I don't deserve her."

The tenderness in his eyes was nearly Macey's undoing. She shifted her feet and searched for the right
words. "You're a great father, Cole. Anyone can see
that. I'm sorry your uncle has you over a barrel. We both
value family. Unfortunately, we're on opposite sides of
this case, trying to protect our own."

Cole's jaw tightened. He dropped his chin to his
chest. "I wish I could make my uncle listen to reason.
He's so insistent on building this strip mall when he
has half a dozen other projects he could be working on.
Before you called, I was at the job site for a new apartment complex along the river."

"You mean the Riverwalk Condos...or whatever
they're called? Those belong to your uncle?"

"Yes." Cole gathered the take-out container and
dropped it in the stainless-steel trash can on the other
side of the sink. "I'd rather see him build more affordable housing, but he wants to offer luxury condos to the
community. Aspen Ridge is a small ranching town. Not
many people could afford the monthly rent, let alone
buy one. But my uncle doesn't see that."

"Why do you work for him again?" Then she winced

and held up a hand. "Sorry—I really need to mind my own business."

He raked a hand over his face. "Quite honestly, right now, I don't even have the time to look for a different position. I'm too busy juggling Wallace's demands while trying to keep Lexi healthy. I'm not doing too hot of a job doing either right now."

"Hey, don't beat yourself up. Ear infections are a normal part of a child's developing years. I had many ear infections as a kid and needed tubes. The antibiotic will kick in soon, and she'll feel like her perky self tomorrow."

"Lexi's not like other kids."

"I disagree. Lexi's very much like other kids. She's able to have a blessed life. Yes, Lexi *is* special. In spite of her NF1. She's special for who she is. She's kind, caring and so sweet." Macey pushed away from the counter and poked him in the chest. "And you're a major part of that. You're raising such a wonderful little girl. I really admire the stellar job you're doing."

"Thanks, that means a lot." Cole grabbed her finger, then wrapped his hand around hers. He took a step closer and looked at her with such light in his eyes that her breath caught. His eyes dropped to her lips.

She swallowed and slowly pulled her hand out of his warm grip. She took a very necessary step back and pulled in a deep breath to steady the rapid pounding against her ribs. She glanced at Lexi who continued to sleep. "Anybody can see how well you're doing. It's gotta be tough doing it on your own though."

"We manage." His voice sounded hoarse.

She returned her attention back to him. "Wyatt knows a thing or two about being a single parent after losing Linnea in childbirth. Like you, he's been raising Mia on his own since the day she was born. And you both had to grieve your losses while parenting a baby. You should check out his support group."

Cole tucked his hands under his arms. "I'll figure things out one way or another. Just hopefully not at the expense of my daughter."

She rested a hand on his shoulder. "Just know you don't have to go it alone."

Cole's phone suddenly vibrated. He pulled it out of his back pocket, glanced at the screen and sighed deeply. Thumbing over the accept button, he answered. "Yeah, Wallace, what's up?"

Macey couldn't make out his uncle's words, especially when Cole turned his back to her, but the way his shoulders bunched and how he dragged a hand over the back of his neck, it couldn't be good.

Cole sighed again. "Well, no, it's not life threatening, but she's got a fever and an infection." He paused as the other man's rumble sounded through the line. "Okay, fine. I'll see what I can do, but no promises. Yeah. Yeah. Okay. Understood." He ended the call and gripped the phone.

Was he about to launch it through the window?

"Everything okay?"

Cole ground his jaw and rolled his neck. "Wallace needs me back at the job site. I need to call my cousin and see if she's available to watch Lexi." He tossed the phone on the counter and dragged his fingers through his hair as he stared into the living room.

"You're working in this weather?"

"We're doing interior work." He sighed. "Man, I really hate to wake her to put her back in the car again."

Macey took two steps toward him and touched his back. "I'll stay."

Cole whirled around so quickly she jumped back. A frown deepened the lines between his eyes. "What?"

"I'll stay with Lexi. Just tell me what time she needs to take her medicine."

Cole lifted his hands. "I don't know when I'll be home. You had her this morning. Plus you have plenty of other things to do. I'll call Piper."

"Piper is just as busy running her business and caring for her own daughter. I planned to spend the full day with her already before we realized she was sick. But if you'd rather take her with you…" Macey lifted a shoulder as she left the rest of her words hanging between them.

Cole heaved a sigh and hung his head. "No, you're right. Thanks. I guess I'm not so great at accepting help."

She lifted an eyebrow. "You think?"

Cole showed Macey the antibiotic and how much to give his daughter. He pocketed his phone and fished out his keys. Then he strode to the living room and brushed a kiss against Lexi's forehead. "I'll be back as quickly as possible. Call if you or Lexi need anything."

Once she closed the door behind him, Macey moved to the recliner. Polly jumped off the couch and into her lap while Lexi continued to sleep soundly.

Sure, she could've used the time to take care of things at the ranch or do more planning for the Sweetheart Ball, but she really felt for the guy who carried the weight of his world on his shoulders.

Clearly, he needed help but was too stubborn to ask.

Her phone buzzed. She pulled it out of her pocket

and saw her twin brother's face on the screen. She answered, "Hey, Bear. What's up?"

"I'm headed into town to file a police report. Can you keep an eye on Tanner and Mia so Wyatt can go with me?"

"Police report?" Her eyes skated to Lexi who struggled to sit up again. "What's going on?"

"While out riding the line, I found some fence posts had been pulled up and tossed. Some trees had been chopped and left lying to rot in the snow. The barn at South Bend's been spray-painted." Bear's voice thundered through the phone line.

"Spray-painted?" Macey groaned and cradled her head in her hand. The Sweetheart Ball is in a couple of weeks. Kind of tough to paint over it in the middle of winter. "Does this have anything to do with Crawford's crew Wyatt had seen on Saturday?"

"When we questioned them, they said they were just looking around. Wyatt and I believed them and reminded them to get permission so they didn't get charged with trespassing."

"Then who could have done it?"

The line went silent. Had their call gotten dropped?"

"Mace, Cole Crawford's hat was found behind the barn along with an empty can of spray paint." Bear's voice lowered to the point where she wasn't quite sure she'd heard correctly."

"Cole? No way. He has enough on his plate without sneaking over to cause damage. Besides, Bear, you know Cole wouldn't do anything like that." A chill slid down the back of her neck. Macey had an idea of who was really responsible.

"Now you're defending the guy?"

Macey turned away from the couch and lowered her voice. "Bear, come on. He's one of your best friends. Of course, I'm defending him. You should be too. He wouldn't hurt any of us on purpose."

"He's involved in taking our land, remember?" Her brother's growl reverberated through the phone.

"He's working for his uncle. That's different."

"Whatever. Can you help or not?"

"I can't. I'm caring for Lexi right now. Where's Mom?"

"She's at the diner, helping Aunt Lynetta. One of the servers called in sick."

"That's right—I was there earlier until Cole needed help again with Lexi."

"All right. I'll see if Ev's home from school. Maybe she can help." Cole blew out a breath. "Listen, it may be best if Cole didn't come around the ranch for a while. Until this thing gets figured out." He hung up before she could protest or even say goodbye.

Macey dropped the phone in her lap and buried her face in her hands.

No matter what happened between her and Cole in the past, she trusted her instincts on this one.

If only she could be in two places at once, but she'd given her word to Cole and couldn't back out. Especially with Lexi being so sick.

Problem was she couldn't shake the betrayal that seeped into her heart from not being able to help her family. Or the way Cole and his daughter were becoming more and more important to her.

She needed to be careful because somebody was going to end up hurt.

"What's wrong, Macey?" Lexi peered behind the curtain of Macey's hair.

She straightened, pushed her hand away from her face and smiled at the little girl standing next to her. Macey pulled the child onto her lap and pressed her lips against Lexi's forehead. Still warm, but not as high as it had been.

"Nothing, sweetheart. How are you feeling?"

Lexi rested her cheek against Macey's chest. "My ear still hurts. But my belly is hungry."

"Would you like some pancakes?"

Lexi sat up and nodded, her feverish eyes bright again.

"Let's warm your food. If you feel up to it, we can play a game or read a story once you're done eating." Lexi scrambled off Macey's lap, then she stood and held her hand out to the little girl.

Lexi took it and they headed into the kitchen. "Okay. Where's Daddy?"

"He's working. That's why I'm here." Macey removed the take-out box from the fridge and retrieved a plate from the cabinet.

"I love you, Macey." Lexi wrapped an arm around Macey's leg.

Blinking back a rush of tears, Macey crouched in front of Lexi and pulled her into her arms. "I love you too, sweet girl."

The more time she spent with Lexi, the less she wanted Cole to find someone more permanent. And her heart would break all over again when she lost another child she loved who wasn't hers.

Cole needed a break, even if it was only for the rest of the evening.

He blew out a breath and rubbed a fist over his sternum, hoping to alleviate the pressure building behind his ribs. With Wallace's attitude getting crankier and his demands increasing, working for him was getting harder.

Knowing Macey would be at his condo when he returned home filled him with more excitement than it should have.

Home.

When was the last time he really considered his condo a home? Sure, he kept it neat and clean for Lexi, but even he could see it lacked a feminine touch.

What would a home be like with her in it?

Don't even go there, man.

He and Macey were just now mending what he'd broken years ago. He wasn't going to do something stupid and destroy their friendship a second time.

As he unlocked the door, music and laughter greeted him. He pushed the door open quietly.

The coffee table, which was covered with a Chutes and Ladders game, a couple of books and a paper pad with an assortment of markers, had been pushed away from the couch. Upbeat children's music blasted from Macey's cell phone. She held on to Lexi's hands, then twirled her, causing more giggles to erupt from his daughter. Then Macey gathered Lexi into her arms and kissed her on the cheek. Polly jumped and barked at their feet.

"Looks like someone's feeling better." He pressed a shoulder against the door frame.

Both heads jerked up. Lexi pushed out of Macey's arms and raced across the room toward him with Polly at her feet. "Daddy! I missed you."

"I missed you too, peanut." He gathered her close,

smelling the scent of her still-damp hair. "You must be feeling better."

Lexi nodded. "Uh-huh. Macey said dance parties always make her feel better, so we tried it. Guess what?"

"What?"

"It did! Macey is so smart." Lexi wriggled out of his arms.

Cole released his daughter, scratched Polly's chin and captured Macey's gaze. "Yes, she is."

Closing the door behind him, he toed off his boots and lined them up next to Macey's. Then he shrugged out of his Carhartt jacket and hung it in the closet next to hers.

Side by side.

Partners. Help mates. What would that be like? With someone like Macey.

No.

With Macey herself.

He ran a hand over his head, smoothing down his hair and moved closer to Macey. "How's it going?"

She shut off her phone and pocketed it. Then she gathered the markers, paper pad and shoved the game pieces into their box. She put everything where it belonged on Lexi's toy shelf. Then she moved the coffee table back in place.

Finally, she straightened and shoved her hands in her front pockets, her arms stiff. She cocked her head, the laughter gone from her eyes. "As you can see, Lexi's feeling a little better. I think it's more from the pain reliever though. She ate her pancakes, took her medicine and had a bath after her fever broke. Then we played a game, read a story, drew pictures and danced to music."

"I'm glad to hear it. Thank you so much. I really appreciate it."

She nodded, then moved past him toward the door. He caught her arm. "Hey, you okay?"

She glanced at his hand and he dropped it. She shook her head. "No, not really."

"What's going on?"

Lexi ran over to her toy shelf and grabbed the paper pad. "Daddy, I drew a picture. Wanna see it?"

"Sure, Lexi Lou." He knelt on one knee in front of her.

She cocked her head and gave him a stern look. "Silly Daddy. I'm Lexi Jane."

He gave a damp curl a little tug. "My mistake."

She pulled out a paper and held it up. "Look. It's you and me and Macey. And I drawed a heart too."

Cole took the picture, his heart twisting. Three stick figures with oversize heads and legs coming out of their necks stood side by side holding very large hands with each other.

"Do you like it?" She bounced on her toes, her eyes wide and eager.

He wrapped an arm around her tiny waist and drew her to him. "I love it. It's the best picture I've ever seen."

"Macey said that too." Lexi threw her arms around his neck, nearly knocking him off balance.

From the corner of his eye, he could see Macey edging closer to the door.

"Hey, squirt. I need to talk to Macey a minute, then we'll put this on the fridge, okay?"

"Okay, Daddy." Lexi dropped the picture on the coffee table, then burrowed under her mermaid blanket. Polly curled up next to her.

He straightened and turned as Macey buttoned her coat and shouldered her tote.

"Hey, what's the rush? I was hoping we could talk for a few minutes. I had an idea for the ball that I wanted to run by you. Why do I sense you're angry at me?"

She crossed her arms, the sweetness she displayed around Lexi dissolved from her face. "Missing anything? A hat perhaps? Maybe some spray paint?"

He cocked his head. "What are you talking about?"

Macey pulled her phone out of her back pocket and pointed it at him. "Bear called and said someone vandalized ranch property. A worn Colorado Rockies hat was found at the scene, along with an empty can of red spray paint."

Cole's eyes widened and he held up his hands. "Mace, I promise you—I had nothing to do with that. But I will look into it and see what I can find out."

He cupped a hand over his eyes. He'd spent so much time at the Riverside Condos job site that he hadn't been in his office much this week. Was his hat still on his desk when he stopped in before he'd headed to the job site? He couldn't remember.

What other surprises were in store for him today?

Her shoulders sagged as she pressed a shoulder against the coat closet door. "That's what I told Bear."

He folded his arms over his chest. "If that's what you thought, then why accuse me?"

Her head lifted, her eyes challenging him. "I didn't accuse—I asked if you were missing anything."

His eyebrow shot up. "Well, your tone and posture are quite accusatory."

"You're right. I'm sorry. It's just this whole land battle is exhausting." Polly pawed at Macey's leg, and she stooped to pick her up. She buried her face in the dog's neck.

"It doesn't have to be."

Macey set Polly on the floor and stood. Her chin lifted as her eyes scraped across his. "If we give in, you mean?"

Cole nodded, even though he knew it wasn't the right answer.

"If we sell, then what do we do when the next developer wants to take a different piece of our ranch? Little by little, we'll be out of a place to live. We need to stop it from happening from the very beginning."

"Sometimes private land is essential for public domain."

"Sure, when it comes to the health and welfare of the community, but a strip mall? Seriously? That's just Wallace being greedy and going after my dad because of a grudge."

"I wish things were different."

"Me, too. When I was at the diner earlier, I was talking to customers. You may be surprised by how many aren't interested in a strip mall and want to help us to preserve the integrity of the ranch." She pulled her gloves and keys out of one of the pockets. "You should know that Bear and Wyatt filed a police report. Your hat is considered evidence. The police may be stopping by to ask some questions."

Cole dragged a hand over his face. "This is not fair. I'm being used as someone else's scapegoat. You realize that, don't you?"

He wasn't about to take the fall for someone else's crime. But more importantly, he didn't want Macey to think he'd do anything to hurt her family or their property for his personal gain.

With her head lowered, Macey nodded. Then she looked at him again, her eyes shadowed. "There's one more thing."

He could only imagine what that could be.

"What?"

"Bear thinks it would be a good idea for you to stay away from the ranch until this thing is settled."

Cole shook his head. "What do *you* think?"

She fiddled with her keys and shrugged. "I don't know. This has me tied in knots. I know you didn't do it, Cole, but I don't trust your uncle at all." She waved a hand over the room. "Maybe it would be a good idea if I cared for Lexi here at your place instead of the ranch."

"Yeah, sure. Whatever. You're always welcome here. You know that. But what about helping with the ball?"

She shrugged again. "Most of the planning is done. It's mostly getting the barn set up and decorated. I'm sure my siblings can lend a hand with that."

Cole held her gaze a moment, then shook his head. "No, I gave you my word, and I'll see it through. I'll help with the setup and all of that. If I need to be escorted onto the property and chaperoned, then so be it. But we are going to finish this together."

"Okay." Macey rested her elbow on the door frame and shoved a hand through her hair. "You mentioned an idea?"

"Oh. Right. I was thinking about another mini fundraiser for the night of the ball. People could buy roses in white, pink, and red, then write notes to their someone special. They will be waiting for them when they arrive. For those who don't receive a rose, I'll buy white ones and write something to encourage them. You may think it's a silly idea, but I got the idea when I drove past the floral shop on my way home."

She smiled for the first time since she became aware of his appearance after returning home. "Actually, I think it's a sweet idea, and I'm not surprised."

"I used to buy my mom a rose every Valentine's Day. I'd ask Lynetta for odd jobs until I had enough money."

Her face softened. "I didn't know that. You loved your mom very much, didn't you?"

He nodded, kicking his socked toe against the carpet. "She was awesome."

"And you're a great dad. Irene Douglas was right—she'd be so proud of you." Macey gave his arm a gentle squeeze, then dropped her hand. She looked over his shoulder, then refocused on him. "How does someone know if they're doing the right thing?"

Even though her question felt rhetorical, he pressed his lips together and lifted a shoulder. "I don't have an answer because I'm wrestling with the same question."

Somehow, he needed to figure out a solution before anyone he cared about got hurt.

Chapter Seven

According to Lexi, pancakes fixed everything.

While she sat in a booth by the door and ate the sprinkle pancakes with whipped cream Lynetta made especially for her, Macey taped a poster advertising the Sweetheart Ball to the glass door.

"Macey, look at me."

She turned away from the door and grinned. "You silly goose. Who put that whipped cream on your nose?"

"I did." The little girl fell back against the booth and giggled.

Macey slid into the booth next to Lexi, grabbed her napkin and wiped it off. "Whipped cream goes in your tummy, not on your nose."

"Can we make a snowman after breakfast?"

"Yep. As soon as you're finished, we'll head to the park."

"What's going on here?" Aunt Lynetta refilled Macey's cup, then set the pot on the table as she slid onto the bench across from them. "How are you feeling, sugar?"

"I'm all better. Daddy and Macey gave me a annabotic that made my ears stop hurting. Guest what,

Netta? We're going to the park to make a snowman."
Lexi clapped her hands and shot Aunt Lynetta a beaming smile.

"A snowman? Well, that sounds like fun." Aunt Lynetta glanced at Macey's untouched ham and cheese omelet. "Something wrong with your breakfast, sweetie?"

Macey picked up her fork and toyed with the food. "Not hungry, I guess. Definitely nothing against Uncle Pete's cooking."

"I know you guys are going through a tough time. Keep your chin up, girl."

"It's getting harder, Aunt Lynetta. I'm trying not to let what happened get me down, but you should've seen how angry Bear and Wyatt were after they came home from the police station. We all know C—" She shot a look at Lexi. "We know you-know-who had nothing to do with it, but they have no other leads at this point. But it's just not that." Macey lowered her head.

Aunt Lynetta reached across the table and grabbed Macey's hand. "What else's going on?"

"After the guys returned to the ranch, they met with the appraiser, but the meeting didn't go as planned. Bear and Wyatt had hoped the land was worth more than what the appraiser had said. They talked about getting a second opinion or something like that. Then this morning, I came in from doing barn chores and found Mom upset about Dad still being in the hospital."

"Your mother is one of the strongest people I know, but all of this worrying has got to be weighing on her. On all of you." Aunt Lynetta stood and reached for the coffeepot.

Being short on help at the diner and worrying about her brother and the problems at the ranch, Aunt Lynetta was also showing signs of fatigue with new lines around her mouth and shadows under her eyes.

"I don't know how to fix any of this." Tears pricked her eyes.

Aunt Lynetta cupped her cheek. "Oh, sweet girl, it's not your job to fix it. Your job is to pray and trust God with the outcome."

"Trusting's so much easier when our lives are running smoothly."

"Amen to that, but then we miss out on the blessings of growing closer to Him."

"What if we pray and trust but don't like the outcome?"

"Even if you don't like the outcome, you have to remember God knows best. He works all things together for good for those who love Him."

"Macey, are you sad?" Lexi rested her head against Macey's arm.

She drew her close and gave her a side hug. "How can I be sad when I get to have breakfast with such a wonderful girl like you?"

Aunt Lynetta nodded toward the door. "I'm so glad you're moving forward with the ball. Would've been a shame if it had been canceled, but no one would've blamed your parents."

Running her fingers over the lettering, she said, "It may be the last one held at South Bend, so Cole and I plan to make it special."

"Speaking of that young man, you two are spending a lot of time together."

"We're friends, Aunt Lynetta. Nothing more. I'm caring for Lexi, and he's helping with the ball. Besides, that's all that can be with us. At least until this land issue is resolved." Macey shoved the roll of tape in her bag along with the rest of the posters she'd had picked up from the printer before heading to the diner.

Aunt Lynetta slung an arm around her shoulders. "God's got this. And your family. Nothing that happens is gonna surprise Him."

Macey rested her head on Aunt Lynetta's shoulder. "I admire your faith."

"Girl, that's the same faith you've grown up with." Aunt Lynetta clicked her tongue. "I know your family's faced a bunch of challenges lately, but you're strong. You guys will get through this." She tapped Macey's chest. "Don't allow your feelings to rule what's in here. God hasn't gone anywhere. Maybe you're the one who put the distance between you and Him."

Leave it to her aunt to tell her like it was.

"I need to get set up for lunch and start my pie baking for this weekend's WinterFest. I've got you. You know that, right?" Aunt Lynetta opened her arms.

Macey slid out of the booth, walked into her embrace, and breathed in the familiar scents of coffee and maple syrup. "Yes, I know. I love you. Thanks for always being in my corner."

Her aunt tipped her chin. "That's a pretty big corner. Once you realize you're not standing in it alone, the better off you'll be."

Allowing those words to linger, she grabbed a to-go box from behind the counter and scraped her untouched omelet into the container.

Lexi finished her milk and wiped her mouth. "I'm done. Can we make a snowman now?"

"Sure, sweetie. Let's get your coat on, then we'll head back to your house to get your snow pants." Macey reached for Lexi's pink jacket and held it out for her.

The little girl jumped up on the bench and shoved her arms in the sleeves.

The bells above the door jangled as it swung open.

Macey turned and swallowed a groan.

Wallace Crawford strode in, a cocky grin on his face. He held a couple of large pieces of torn paper with colors that matched her posters.

"Good morning, Ms. Stone." His eyes narrowed as he tipped his hat.

Macey moved in front of the booth, placing herself between the shark and his great-niece. Her eyes raked over the papers in his hand. "Mr. Crawford. Destroy anyone else's property today?"

He raised an eyebrow, that smug grin back in place. "Whatever are you referring to, little lady?"

"Drop that patronizing tone with me. I'm not afraid of you. My family's working with the police, and soon, you will be held accountable for your actions."

His gray eyes hardened and glinted like polished steel. He lifted his beefy paw clutching the papers. "You really think a silly ball is going to help people get behind saving your ranch?"

"Maybe they will if you stop tearing down the posters. Feeling threatened?"

He threw his head back and laughed, the sound bouncing off the walls and drawing attention to him still blocking the doorway. "Hardly. Once people see what the city council has designed, they'll be waiting in line to dig up the property to get the project moving even faster. I heard about your bit of bad luck. Maybe your family should accept the council's offer and stop dragging this out so nothing else happens to the ranch you're crusading to save."

"I don't believe in luck. I know you're responsible for the vandalism, and we're going to prove it. And you underestimate this town. They love our family. They believe in community. This strip mall isn't the first big box retailer they've shut down." Macey pressed her fingers against the table and hoped the bravado in her voice didn't betray the skepticism she was beginning to feel in her heart.

"Maybe not, but it sure will be the last. Especially when I offer them more opportunities for shopping and dining beyond this dump." He waved his hand across the diner.

"Wallace Crawford, I heard that." Aunt Lynetta rounded the counter with fire in her eyes. She stared at him with one hand fisted on her hip and the other waving toward the door. "Your money's no good here anymore. Just turn around and get your coffee somewhere else."

"Oh, Lynetta. When the strip mall opens, you're going to be begging me to bring customers back to this dive."

"You can threaten me all you want and have the audacity to pretend you're innocent in destroying my family's property, but the truth will come out. You think a fancy coffee shop will shut down the diner my parents started over fifty years ago? You're welcome to try. In the meantime, get off my property and stay off it."

Wallace shook his head and tossed the torn poster on the floor. "I have more important things to do with my time anyway." He tipped his hat. "Good day, ladies."

The bell above the door clanged as he slammed it on the way out.

Face heated and heart racing, Macey turned her back

to the diners who had watched the show. She zipped Lexi's jacket and helped her pull on her mittens. "Sorry about the drama, Aunt Lynetta."

Her aunt squeezed her arm. "Don't allow him to get under your skin."

"Thanks for sticking up for me. I talked tough, but my stomach turned to jelly."

"Oh, girl, you're so much stronger than you think. And you did well not to cower under that man's intimidation."

"Maybe so, but I can't help but wonder what else he has in store for my family. Or even Cole and Lexi."

"That's what galls me the most." Her aunt nodded toward Lexi who picked up Macey's phone. "He's dangling that precious child's health in front of her daddy like a carrot."

"Isn't there something we could do to help them?"

Aunt Lynetta sighed. "Darlin', I've tried. Believe me. But Cole has his mama's blood rushing through his veins. That woman was my best friend, but she was the most stubborn person I'd ever met. She wouldn't accept a handout if someone glued it to her fingers. Cole's grandparents accused her of being a gold digger when she and Edward had gotten married. After he passed away, she insisted on making her own way and drilled the same into Cole."

"But there are programs that could help Lexi and release Cole from under Wallace's thumb."

"I hear you and appreciate your heart, but Cole has to be the one to accept it. In the meantime, he'll keep allowing Wallace to pull his strings until he gets so tangled that he's ready to cut them himself. And I'll be the first in line to hand him the scissors and give him all the help he needs. He's like the child Pete and I couldn't have."

"I admire what he's doing by caring for Lexi on his own."

Aunt Lynetta raised an eyebrow. "Just how much admiring is going on there?"

Macey rolled her eyes. "Don't even go there. Like I told you—Cole's just a friend. But I do feel for his situation and wish I could do something other than talking my family into accepting Crawford's offer to help him."

"The pancakes you delivered, then caring for Lexi while he had to go back to work, sure helped."

"That sweet child shouldn't have to suffer because of adult issues. I did what anyone else would have done."

"Not anyone else and you know it." Aunt Lynetta brushed a thumb across Macey's cheekbone. "And from the moment Cole was mentioned, your lovely skin has taken on a rosy glow."

She pushed her aunt's hand away and shook her head. "You're imagining things."

Aunt Lynetta laughed, a sound that warmed Macey from the inside out, even if it was directed at her. "I don't think so, girl, but time will tell. Then I'll be the first to whisper, 'I told you so.'"

Macey pressed a hand to her face, not surprised to feel the warmth. She did not have time to fall for the guy and his adorable daughter. So how could she protect her heart from getting destroyed in the process?

Being a grown man with a daughter, Cole really hated the feeling of being thirteen all over again and being summoned to the principal's office.

Wallace's door slamming and thunderous shouting

of Cole's name from across the hall made his stomach clench.

He ended his phone call and grabbed the land appraisal file off the corner of his desk. Blowing out a breath, he stiffened his spine and rapped two knuckles on Wallace's open door. "Ready for our meeting?"

Wallace looked up from his computer screen, a scowl deepening the lines in his weathered face. "What are you talking about?"

"We had a scheduled meeting forty-five minutes ago to review Leland Stebbins's appraisal."

"You sure?"

"You set the meeting yourself."

With his elbow propped on his desk, Wallace ran a hand over his forehead. "Okay, fine. Get in here and shut the door."

Again feeling like a kid in trouble, Cole did as demanded, then sat in one of the chairs across from his uncle's desk. He opened the folder and pulled out the appraisal report.

Wallace reached across the desk, snatched the papers from Cole's hand and skimmed them, then tossed them back across the desk. "I don't like those numbers. We need another appraisal done. This time, go with Vinny Montrose."

"The council voted against using his services and went with Stebbins instead."

"Just do as you're told and call him. The sooner we can get this one done, the quicker we can sit down with the Stones and hash out a price."

Cole swallowed a sigh and stood. "Sure, whatever you want."

"What I want is for you to get that Stone family to

accept the offer so we can move forward. Stop cozying up to the daughter and do the job I'm paying you to do."

And there it was.

Somehow his uncle would make this his fault.

"I've done everything I'm supposed to do. Despite what you think, I haven't been dragging my feet on this." Cole reached for the scattered papers and stacked them together before sliding them back into his folder. He started for the door, then turned back to his uncle who'd tuned him out and shifted his focus to the computer. "By the way, you know anything about my missing hat?"

"Hat? What hat? Do I look like your mother?"

"The one that's been sitting on my desk since I started working here. Dad bought it when he took me to a Rockies game."

"It's not my job to keep track of your stuff." Wallace waved him away.

Cole stalked back to his uncle's desk. "My hat came up missing. Then, it was found on Stone River where the property had been vandalized."

Wallace leaned back in his chair and tossed up his hands. "So if you know where your hat is, then why are you asking me about it?"

"*I* haven't been on that section of the property." He jerked a thumb toward his chest. "*I* didn't remove my hat from my desk."

Wallace's eyes glinted as he pushed to his feet. Bracing his fingers on his desk, he leaned forward until he was less than six inches from Cole's face. "What are you accusing me of, son?"

Cole refused to direct his gaze away. His jaw tightened. "First, I'm not your son. Second, I'm simply ask-

Get up to 4
FREE FABULOUS BOOKS
in your welcome box!

To thank you for being a loyal reader we'd like to send you up to 4 FREE BOOKS, absolutely free when you try the Harlequin Reader Service.

Just write "YES" on the Loyal Reader Voucher and we'll send you your welcome box with 2 free books from each series you choose plus free mystery gifts! Each welcome box is worth over $20.

Try **Love Inspired® Romance Larger-Print** and get 2 books and fall in love with inspirational romances that take you on an uplifting journey of faith, forgiveness and hope.

Try **Love Inspired® Suspense Larger-Print** and get 2 books where courage and optimism unite in stories of faith and love in the face of danger.

Or **TRY BOTH** **and get 2 books from each series!**

Your welcome box is completely free, even the shipping! If you continue with your subscription, you can look forward to curated monthly shipments of brand-new books from your selected series, always at a discount off the cover price! Plus you can cancel any time.

So don't miss out, return your Loyal Readers Voucher today to get your Free Welcome Box.

Pam Powers

LOYAL READER
FREE BOOKS VOUCHER
WELCOME BOX

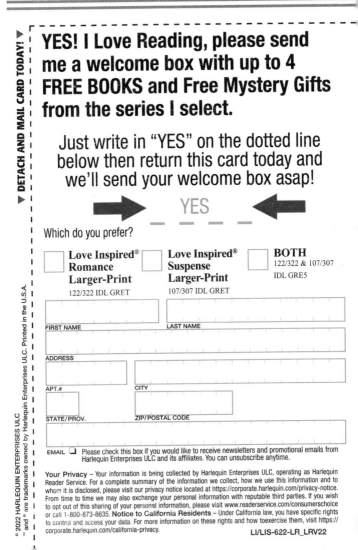

◄ DETACH AND MAIL CARD TODAY! ▼

YES! I Love Reading, please send me a welcome box with up to 4 FREE BOOKS and Free Mystery Gifts from the series I select.

Just write in "YES" on the dotted line below then return this card today and we'll send your welcome box asap!

➡ _ _ YES _ _ _ _ ⬅

Which do you prefer?

☐ **Love Inspired® Romance Larger-Print**
122/322 IDL GRET

☐ **Love Inspired® Suspense Larger-Print**
107/307 IDL GRET

☐ **BOTH**
122/322 & 107/307
IDL GRE5

FIRST NAME

LAST NAME

ADDRESS

APT.#

CITY

STATE/PROV.

ZIP/POSTAL CODE

EMAIL ☐ Please check this box if you would like to receive newsletters and promotional emails from Harlequin Enterprises ULC and its affiliates. You can unsubscribe anytime.

Your Privacy – Your information is being collected by Harlequin Enterprises ULC, operating as Harlequin Reader Service. For a complete summary of the information we collect, how we use this information and to whom it is disclosed, please visit our privacy notice located at https://corporate.harlequin.com/privacy-notice. From time to time we may also exchange your personal information with reputable third parties. If you wish to opt out of this sharing of your personal information, please visit www.readerservice.com/consumerschoice or call 1-800-873-8635. **Notice to California Residents** – Under California law, you have specific rights to control and access your data. For more information on these rights and how to exercise them, visit https://corporate.harlequin.com/california-privacy.

LI/LIS-622-LR_LRV22

▲ If offer card is missing write to: Harlequin Reader Service, P.O. Box 1341, Buffalo, NY 14240-8531 or visit www.ReaderService.com ▲

ing if you know anything about it. Seems strange that my hat would show up at that site without me being there. I won't take the fall for something I didn't do."

"Maybe you need to be more careful with your things." Wallace straightened and folded his hands over his chest.

Cole slapped the folder against his uncle's desk. "I had nothing to do with that vandalism, and you know it."

"Do I now?"

"Wallace, I am doing my best to move forward with this project, but I will not get caught up in your schemes." He stared at his uncle.

The man was impossible.

Cole dropped his chin to his chest, shook his head and pulled in a breath. "If you're so unhappy with my work performance, then maybe you should start looking for my replacement."

"I've been considering that for a while now. But let me remind you—you owe me. Who took care of you after your mama died? Paid for your fancy private school and college tuition? Who replaced those rags you wore with brand names?" He jerked a thumb to his chest. "You had nothing before me, and don't you forget it."

Cole ground his jaw as he looked at his expensive polished shoes. Then he lifted his head and skated his gaze over his uncle's smug face. "How can I forget it when you continually remind me? But you're wrong. I had everything until my mother died. Then I was left with nothing. I've been repaying my tuition every month since I've started working for you. That debt is nearly paid. Once that's done, then so are we."

"Have you forgotten about the little thing called insurance? How will you care for that little brat?"

Cole rounded the desk and gripped his hands into fists to prevent from reaching for his uncle's shirt collar. "Don't you ever talk about my daughter that way again."

Wallace shoved him back and gripped the lapels of his own leather sport coat. "I'll talk about her any way I see fit, and there's nothing you can do about it. So you'd better watch your tongue and get back to doing your job."

Cole stalked back to his own office and slammed the door, his adrenaline surging. He paced in front of his desk, feeling caged in the windowless room. Then he yanked his phone out of his back pocket and thumbed through his contacts until he found Wyatt Stone's information. He tapped on the number and waited for his childhood friend to pick up.

"Hey, Cole. What's up?" A child cried in the background.

"Hey, man. You got a minute?"

"Maybe about half that, actually. Mia's having a meltdown at that moment because I won't let her drink from the dog's water dish."

In spite of the rage coiled in his stomach, Cole couldn't hold back a laugh. "Been there with the tantrums, man. Listen, I wondered if we could meet. I need to ask a favor."

"Sure, dude. Not a problem. Care to swing by the cabin?"

"I'll be there in fifteen minutes."

"See you then." The line ended, and for the first time, Cole could breathe.

Fifteen minutes later, he kicked the snow off his

boots as he stood on the full-length covered porch and knocked on Wyatt's cabin door. Inside, a dog barked and footsteps raced across the floor.

The door opened. A toddler with red-rimmed eyes and half of her hair in one ponytail while the other half stuck to her face stared at him without saying a word. A black-and-white spotted English setter nosed around the little girl.

Cole dropped to his haunches and held his palm out as the dog sniffed his fingers while directing his attention to the child. "Hey, you must be Mia. Is your daddy home?"

The little girl nodded and ran away, leaving the door open. The dog barked and chased after her, leaving Cole alone at the door.

He straightened and peered inside. "Wyatt?"

His friend hurried into the large open room with a dish towel over his shoulder and a cup in one hand. "Hey, man. Come in. Sorry about that. I was filling Mia's cup when you arrived."

"You sure this isn't a bad time?" Cole stepped inside and closed the door. He scuffed his feet on the rug in the entryway.

He took in the exposed log walls and the crackling fire warming the room from the stone fireplace that went to the ceiling. A navy and rust braided rug lay in front of a rust-colored couch and matching chair. A large flatscreen mounted on the wall above the mantel. Framed pictures of Wyatt in dress blues with his arms around a dark-haired woman wearing a wedding gown and one of Wyatt holding his daughter hung on either side of the fireplace.

Colorful dishes and plastic food spilled out of the play kitchen set in the corner of the room.

"Cool digs."

"Thanks. Used to be an old foreman cabin, but I've been fixing it up. It's big enough for Mia and me to call home. So, what's up?"

Cole shoved his hands in his trouser pockets. "I know I have no right asking this, but I need help, and I don't know where else to turn."

Wyatt scooped up a remote, a doll and a book about farm animals off one of the couch cushions, then waved for Cole to sit. "Sure, whatever you need. Have a seat."

Cole sat on the edge of the couch, balanced his elbows on his knees and clasped his hands. "First, I want you to know I had nothing to do with your family's property being destroyed."

Wyatt slumped in the overstuffed chair and rested his right ankle on his left knee. "I didn't think that for a minute."

Cole shared his recent confrontation with his uncle, then dragged a hand over his face. "I think he's dirty, but I can't prove it. You mentioned one of the guys in your single father support group was a private investigator?"

"Yes, Barry Harrelson. He's a retired cop who works with the Stone River PD on an as needed basis."

"Mind giving me his contact info or maybe set up a meeting with him?"

Wyatt pulled out his phone. His thumbs tapped across the screen. Seconds later, Cole's phone vibrated in his pocket. "I sent you his contact information. I'll text him and tell him to expect your call."

"Thanks, man. I appreciate it."

"Sure thing. We single dads need to stick together, right?" Wyatt eyed him. "You okay?"

Cole exhaled. "I'm about to be canned, I think. I've been holding on to this job because of Lexi, but honestly, being out from under Wallace's thumb may be a blessing."

Wyatt leaned forward and clapped a hand on Cole's shoulder. "Whatever you need, I'm here to help you through it. Just ask."

Ask.

So much easier said than done.

Chapter Eight

Wyatt's words stuck with Cole as he stood at the checkout at Regals Shoes.

What would it be like to have someone like Wyatt in his corner? Someone who understood the struggles of single parenting? Maybe he should check out that support group after all. He'd worry about that later. Right now he needed to check out and head back to work for a bit.

Yesterday, while getting Lexi ready for her follow-up at the pediatrician, she'd mentioned her shoes pinching her toes.

He'd come in to find Mrs. Regal marking down shoes and adding them to the clearance sale rack. After finding a pair of regular-priced brand-name shoes for Lexi, he'd cleared the clearance sale rack of kids' shoes and carried the boxes to the front register until the display was empty.

Cole understood poverty and sacrifice. Until he had gone to live with Wallace after his mother's death, going without had been the norm.

Getting shoes for his daughter had been his priority, but the great sale on the shoes gave him an opportunity to pay it forward and help some other kid from feeling less than.

"Your mama would be proud of you, young man. Hope you know that." White-haired Mrs. Regal peered over the top of her glasses at him as she directed her scanner gun at another barcode.

"It's for a good cause." He eyed the growing stack of boxes. The total would still be less than the amount he spent on one pair of his own work boots, especially with the deep discounts she had marked.

"And you and your big heart, young man."

The front door opened, and Mrs. Regal looked up from her register. "Hey, Nora." Then her eyes widened. She dropped the scanner gun, rushed around the counter and hurried to the door, her arms outstretched. She wrapped Macey in a hug that nearly knocked the young woman off her feet.

"Macey Stone. Young lady, you are a sight for this old woman's eyes. I heard you were back in town and hoped you'd stop in sometime."

"Hey, Marla. How are you doing?"

"Sugar, I can't complain. The good Lord watches over and protects me every day." She released Macey and hustled back to the counter. "You two look around and I'll be with you as soon as I'm done ringing up Cole here."

"We just found the most wonderful dresses for the ball, and we're looking for shoes to go with them."

Cole's heart jerked at the sound of Macey's voice. He gripped the counter and tried not to let his eyes linger over the way Macey's hair brushed against her red wool jacket.

He straightened as she headed to the counter, her eyebrows raised as she took in the multiple bulging bags at his feet. "Someone has a shoe weakness."

Then she shot him a grin that nearly dissolved him into a puddle.

Get a grip, man.

Cole smirked and reached for a navy sneaker covered in white daisies. "Not quite my size."

"Lexi's going to be thrilled with so many pairs of shoes."

"I admit to spoiling my daughter, but not like this."

Ms. Marla scanned the final pair of shoes on the counter and read him the total. "Cole, bless his heart, buys up children's shoes and boots when I put them on clearance sale and donates them to the local day care centers and elementary school for kids who can't afford them."

Heat scalded his neck as he pulled out his wallet. "Mrs. Regal, that was our secret, remember?"

The older woman clapped a hand over her mouth, then took his bank card. "I'm sorry, love. It's just such a good thing you're doing.

Macey touched his elbow and looked at him with almost a wonder in her eyes. "That's very sweet, Cole. What a kind and generous thing to do."

He lifted a shoulder and scrawled his name at the bottom of the receipt. "I'm just paying forward what someone had done for me."

"Someone bought shoes for you?"

"Once, when I was ten." That moment still rubbed a raw edge around his heart.

Carrying a box, Mrs. Stone joined Macey. She shot

him a wide smile full of kindness. "Hi, Cole. It's good to see you again."

He nodded to her, wondering if she overheard their conversation. "Hey, Mrs. Stone. Good to see you as well. How's Mr. Stone doing?"

"He's being discharged this evening. Macey and I had a few errands to run, then we're going to pick him up. How's that sweet daughter of yours?"

"Lexi's doing well. She's nearly recovered from a double ear infection." He glanced at his watch. "She's spending the night with my cousin and her daughter."

Mrs. Stone slipped her arm around his shoulders and gave him a quick squeeze. "Give her a hug from me. I miss seeing her at the ranch, but I'll see her on Sunday for children's church."

"Will do. She loves listening to your stories. All the way home from church, she rattles on about what Miss Nora taught her. Last week was all about the big fish who swallowed the man who ran away."

Mrs. Stone laughed. "They were really into the Jonah story and the puppets we made. I'm so glad she enjoys it. She's a gem, and we're so thankful to have her. Both of you."

"Thank you." Her words touched him more than he could say. He lifted three of the bags. "Mrs. Regal, I'll be back in a minute for the rest."

"I can help." Before he could protest, Macey took the remaining two bags off the counter and nodded toward the door. "You lead, and I'll follow."

He walked backward and pushed open the door with his shoulder, then held it while Macey passed, her scent wreathing him.

Out on the sidewalk, he pulled in a lungful of crisp

air, then nodded to his truck parked across the street. "I'm over there."

They paused at the corner for the crosswalk signal to change.

"Just when I thought I had you figured out, you surprise me, Cole."

He eyed Macey, then watched the light turn from red to green. "Let's walk. How do I surprise you?"

"I don't know. Stuff like this." She hefted the bags. "Who does that?"

He couldn't see her eyes through her oversize sunglasses, but the way her lips tipped up made him think she wasn't passing judgment. In fact, her words carried a tone of respect.

He lifted a shoulder, wishing they could change the subject. He shifted all the bags to one hand so he could pull out his key fob and unlock the truck. "Someone who doesn't want other kids to be teased about holes in their shoes."

She set the bags on the back seat, then lifted her sunglasses onto her head, holding back her hair. She stuffed her gloved hands in her pockets. "I'm sorry you had to go through that. Kids can be so cruel. When we were younger, my mom told us about this one time she'd gone into Regals. A little boy was so excited to buy a new pair of shoes, but he didn't have enough money, so she paid the balance. She said she'd never seen anyone so excited over a pair of shoes before. She'd remind us of the story when we whined about wanting something we really didn't need."

Cole shoved his bags next to the ones Macey placed in the back. "Yeah, I'm quite familiar with the story."

Macey's eyes widened. "You are?"

He shoved his hands in his front pockets and kicked a clump of salted snow off his tire. "I'm the kid she was talking about."

"Oh." Her single word almost whispered spoke volumes. "I'm sorry if I embarrassed you."

He laughed, but the decades-old humiliation resurfaced, reminding him of where he'd come from and how he needed to be the one to make his way in the world. "We all have our wounds, right?"

"And that's why you donate shoes." Her voice soft and gentle, Macey gripped his upper arm. "You really are amazing, Cole Crawford."

Cole looked at her fingers on his arm and forced his heart to beat steadily against his rib cage. A woman touching him shouldn't create this type of reaction. Was he that hard up for attention?

But Macey wasn't just any woman. The more he was around her, the more he wanted to touch her, pull her close.

But he couldn't.

Not as long as they were on opposing sides—both desperately trying to get what they wanted for their families. Her family who had been nothing but good to him.

"Hey, have the police learned anything else about the vandalism?"

Macey shook her head. "Not that I know of. Bear and Wyatt removed the spray paint and hosed down the barn with the power washer, so it won't be an eyesore for the ball. You still planning to sell tickets with me tomorrow at WinterFest?"

Cole gripped the back of his neck. "Yes. What time do you want me there?"

"Is nine too early? We'll have a table set up in the

food hall. It's out of the elements and receives pretty decent traffic with people getting coffee and something to eat."

He shook his head. "No. I was planning to meet Piper around noon anyway."

"Great. Sounds good. I'll see you later. I need to find shoes for the dress I bought." She headed back to the crosswalk. As she walked to the shoe store, Cole longed to chase after her and invite her out to dinner. Or something. Anything so he didn't have to return to the condo by himself.

But he couldn't. Even if the land deal divided them. She came from such a great family. And he...well, he didn't deserve Macey.

And the more he remembered that, the better off he'd be.

Macey wouldn't let her aunt down.

She couldn't say no when Aunt Lynetta called with the plea in her voice. Even if it meant Macey tamping down the panic pressing against her ribs.

With WinterFest tomorrow, the last thing Aunt Lynetta needed was an unexpected trip to the ER after slicing her hand while peeling apples.

With her brothers working the ranch, Everly caring for Tanner and Mia and Mom caring for Dad at the ranch house, that left Macey to finish the baking for tomorrow's pie auction.

Aunt Lynetta's pies were legendary in Aspen Ridge. The pie auction raised money each year for the local animal shelter.

Macey could do this.

Although her aunt seldom followed a recipe, her

apple pie was the same one Macey's grandma and mom used. And like the other women in her family, she'd memorized it years ago.

Even if Macey hadn't baked a pie since before her grandma had been killed, it had to be like riding a bike, right? Except she didn't have to worry about skinned knees if she failed.

Just her aunt's reputation.

She glanced at the remaining eight pie plates filled with the bottom crusts. She tugged a yellow Netta's Diner apron over her head and secured the ties in front of her. She reached for a paring knife and grabbed one of the washed apples from the deep sink.

For the next fifteen minutes, she peeled, cored and sliced apples while humming along with the country tunes streaming from the local radio station in the background. With the diner closed and the front of house locked, dark and quiet, Macey soaked in the calm.

Outside, snow drifted down in a whisper. The forecast called for two to four inches overnight, which would be great for the dogsled teams, downhill tubing races and general atmosphere for the WinterFest.

Her phone dinged. She rinsed her hands, reached for it, and found a text from Cole on her lock screen: Hey, tried to call Wyatt but got his voice mail. Wondered if your fam had a vet you'd rec.

Macey didn't have time to tap it all out. She touched his name on her screen and waited while the call rang through.

"Hey, Macey. I just texted you."

"Yes, I saw. I'm up to my elbows in peeling apples, so it was easier to talk on speakerphone."

"Apples? What are you doing?"

"Aunt Lynetta cut her hand. Uncle Pete took her to the ER for stitches. She needs pies made for tomorrow, so here I am." She slivered the remaining apple half and slid it off her silicon cutting board into the glass bowl to be mixed with sugar, cinnamon and lemon juice.

"Want a hand?"

Her fingers stilled as her heart jumped. She swallowed and paused a second. "A hand?"

"Sure, I know my way around a paring knife. I used to make pies with my mom all the time."

"Um, sure. Yeah, great. Consider yourself recruited. Come to the back door."

What was she thinking, agreeing to his request?

"Be there in ten."

Macey ended the call, then rummaged through her tote bag and grabbed her small makeup case. She rushed to the restroom and tugged her hair from the sloppy ponytail she'd tied before entering the kitchen. She brushed her hair and twisted it into a tidier messy bun, pulling a few loose hairs around her face. She swiped on mascara, brushed a little powder on her face, then applied a sheer lip gloss.

Then she made a face at herself in the mirror. What was she doing? This wasn't a date.

Far from it.

"Girl, you are ridiculous," she said out loud.

She returned to the kitchen, tossed her case back in her bag and washed her hands.

A quiet knock sounded on the back door. Macey's fingers tightened around the paring knife as her breath caught in her chest.

Knock it off.

Macey hurried down the small hallway past the diner

office, storage room and industrial cooler. She pushed open the back door.

Cole bounced on the balls of his feet. He flashed a smile.

A smile that warmed her against the burst of cold that accompanied him as he stepped inside and pulled the door shut against the wind. "Man, it's freezing out there."

"Late January in Colorado tends to be that way."

He flashed her another smile. Snowflakes melted on his head, causing his dark brown hair to glisten in the overhead lights.

Macey took a step forward, then caught herself. Seriously? Did she actually plan to brush the wetness off his hair?

Get a grip!

Macey spun away, giving herself a swift mental kick, and didn't wait to see if he was going to follow.

She returned to the sink and reached for another apple. Cole propped a hip against the industrial prep sink and pushed his sleeves up on his charcoal sweater. "Okay, boss. Put me to work."

Forcing herself not to breathe in the spicy scent of his cologne or body wash or whatever he wore, she nodded toward the knives mounted on the magnetic strip above the prep sink. "There's another paring knife there. I've washed the apples. I'm peeling them into this glass bowl, then I'll make the top crusts and bake them."

"How many pies are left to make?"

"Eight. She made half a dozen triple berry pies, three lemon meringue and three chocolate silk. Then she cut her hand and called me in to finish."

"Piece of cake. Or pie, I guess." He shot her a lop-sided half grin that sent her stomach into a spiral.

"Har. Har."

Cole reached for an apple, the back of his hand brushing against her arm.

What was her problem?

She'd been around Cole many times over the past few weeks. So why was she suddenly acting like a high schooler with her first crush?

"Where's Lexi this evening?"

"Piper and Avery took her to a movie. Then, they're having a sleepover."

"Oh, right. You mentioned her spending the night this morning at Regals. Fun for her and a little break for you."

He lifted a shoulder. "It's too quiet without her. I did some work, but then I remembered I needed to make a vet appointment for Polly. I called the one Mrs. Douglas at the shelter had given me, but they're not accepting new patients right now. I tried Wyatt first, then called you."

"He and Bear are working on a busted water line in the barn. Everly's caring for Tanner and Mia. Mom's making sure Dad doesn't overdo it. And I'm here." Then she gave him a sheepish smile as she sprinkled cinnamon over the full bowl of apples. "I guess you didn't need a play-by-play of the Stone family activities. Regardless, that's why Wyatt didn't pick up."

"I like hearing about your family. You're very blessed to have siblings. Being an only child can be lonely at times, especially with no parents around either. Piper's like a sister, but her priorities are Avery and her housecleaning business, as they should be."

Cole peeled his apple in one continuous motion without breaking the skin.

Macey did a mental calculation of how much lemon juice to add to the mix, then eyeballed the measuring cup as she poured. "Yes, I can understand that, especially after being away from my family."

"Mind if I ask what brought you back?" Cole stretched out the long peel, then beginning at one end, he curled the peel together. Then he tucked the bottom end under, placed it on his palm and held an apple peel rose out to her. "For you."

"Look at you, Mr. Creativity." Grinning, she wiped her hands on her apron, then took it. "No one's given me an apple rose before."

"My mom showed me how to make them when I was a kid. Everyone needs a talent. I guess that one's mine."

Oh, he had more than one.

"Your mom made the best Dutch apple pie."

"Yes, she did." He nudged her. "And you didn't answer me."

She could've pretended she didn't know what he was talking about, but Cole deserved better than that. She brushed her thumb over the top of the apple rose, then lifted a shoulder. "My employer hit on me, and his wife walked in on us. She fired me on the spot."

"What do you mean he hit on you?" His voice lowered to a growl.

Macey exhaled, turned and pressed her back against the edge of the sink, the apple rose cupped in her hand. "After college, I spent six years nannying for the Crane family. My college roommate was Tricia Crane's niece, and she said her aunt was looking for a nanny. The pay was good, so I accepted."

"Because of me."

Macey slid the apple rose onto the edge of her cutting board, then rinsed her hands. "Maybe at first. I had agreed to go to prom with you because you and your girlfriend had broken up and you said you weren't getting back together with her. Then she knocked my punch cup out of my hand and it flew all over her dress. She claimed I threw punch on her on purpose and threatened her. When the chaperones asked what had happened, you didn't say anything. I was humiliated when they made me leave—the senior prom I'd spent months planning. Looking back on it now, it was ridiculous mean girl drama. But I just wanted to get away."

Cole's knife clattered against the prep counter. He grabbed Macey's hands, his fingers wet and sticky from apple juice. "I'm so sorry, Macey. I wish I could rewind time and stand up for you the way you deserved. I wanted to fit in and ended up losing the one person who always believed in me."

"I forgave you a long time ago, Cole. It's in the past. Going to college and working for the Cranes allowed me time away. I loved Jayden, Jenna and Jaxson. When I met them, Derek and Tricia seemed to be an ideal couple. When they hired me, Jayden was two, and Tricia was pregnant with Jenna. Things were going well until recently."

"When your employer hit on you?"

Macey nodded. Heat crawled across her face as the events of that night flickered through her mind.

"What happened?"

Macey shot a look at Cole. His eyes drifted back to the apple he sliced, but a muscle jumped in the side of his face as his jaws clenched.

"I'd put the kids to bed when Derek returned from a business meeting or something. He'd been drinking. I didn't expect him to return as early as he did. I was reading in the living room. He'd gone upstairs to check on them, which was normal. Then he came back downstairs and sat next to me on the couch. He tried to kiss me. I tried to push him away, but he was stronger than me. Tricia walked in and when she asked what was going on, he said I was the one who had come on to him. She wouldn't listen to me, demanded I pack my things and be out before the children woke up the next morning. I'd never packed so quickly in all my life. I was on the road within two hours, humiliation chasing me all the way back to the ranch."

"I'm so sorry, Macey. It shouldn't have been like that. You didn't press charges, I take it?"

Macey filled her lungs, then blew out a breath. Her vision blurred as that night replayed in her head. "I didn't see the point. Without any witnesses, it was my word against his. Again, I feared no one would believe me."

"You're home now. And safe. No one will take advantage of you like that again."

"You don't know that. I hope to find someone whom I can trust, who will stick up for me when necessary and stand by my side like my parents do for each other. After taking care of other people's children, I'd love to raise a family on South Bend since it was supposed to be mine someday. But now that may not happen."

"I didn't realize it was part of your inheritance."

She nodded, her eyes awash with more tears. "Not technically. Grandpa knew how much I loved it and said it would be mine. No matter how far I go, South Bend will always be my favorite place on the planet. So many wonderful memories of growing up near my grandparents, riding with my grandpa to the waterfalls, learning how to take pictures, baking with my grandma."

"Sounds like the perfect childhood."

"It was. Problem was, I didn't appreciate it like I should have. I wanted more than the fenced-in pastures of Stone River. Then I found out the grass isn't always greener on the other side of the fence. Just a different type of manure was being spread."

Cole laughed, a deep timbre that bounced off the kitchen walls. Then he sobered. "I'm sorry for my role in jeopardizing your dream."

Macey shook her head. "It's not your fault. I still feel like your uncle is doing it to get back at my dad. My parents keep saying if God wants us to keep our land, then He'll make it happen."

Even if that meant ending up with a broken heart.

Cole certainly didn't mind the unexpected change to his evening. He'd hesitated in texting Macey. Now he was happy he did. Even if peeling apples and the sweet scents of sugar and cinnamon took him back to baking with his mom.

"You got quiet. Regretting your invitation to help?" Macey patted the pie dough into a circle, floured the rolling pin, and rolled it out. She transferred the dough over the filled pie plate, then slid it over to Cole.

"Nah. Just thinking about my mom for a minute."

"You said you and your mom used to bake."

Cole crimped the edges of the dough between his thumbs and forefingers. He cut slits in the crust, then brushed an egg wash across the top. He carried the pie to the oven and slid it on the rack. "One year, we spent an afternoon baking pies as gifts for our neighbors. Everyone wanted to know the secret to Mom's crust because it was always so light and flakey."

"So what was the secret?"

He eyed her and shook his head. "I don't know if I can trust you…"

"Come on… I'm not asking for military secrets." She nudged him as she rinsed a dishcloth in the sink and wiped off the prep counter.

"Well, that's good because I don't have any." He enjoyed laughing together the way they used to. "Actually, my mom added vodka to her dough. She said it kept it moist and from getting tough. Something about it doesn't cause the gluten to form. I don't remember exactly. The only time we had booze in the house was when Mom was baking."

"Sounds like a wonderful memory."

"It was. After we delivered the pies, we created a blanket fort in the living room and watched *Aladdin* on a DVD, which she'd borrowed from the library. For Christmas, she'd given me a knitted hat and scarf that she'd made, which I still have, and bought me a second-hand handheld video game. I loved the time we spent together without her rushing off to another job to help make ends meet."

"Your mom was a hard worker."

"She was. But she was also kind and generous, quick to give up whatever we had for someone else who she felt needed it more."

"I can see where you get it. Especially the shoe thing. Those kids were blessed by your generosity."

Cole gripped the edge of the sink and dropped his

gaze to his feet, warm inside his expensive leather boots. "One time when I was around ten or so, we played basketball during gym class. Every time I ran, the ripped sole of my shoe kept slapping against the floor. I tripped and skinned my knee. My gym teacher offered to duct tape my shoe, and the kids in my class laughed at me, calling me Slappy. I hated it. After school, I walked past Regals. They advertised a huge sale. I found these awesome kicks in my size and took them to the counter, so excited not to be teased again. I had two wrinkly five-dollar bills I'd saved from birthday money. I planned to use one five to buy my mom some nice-smelling lotion for her chapped hands. Mrs. Regal wasn't working. Otherwise, I figure those shoes would've been on sale for five bucks. I'll never forget the look of pity from the teenage cashier when she said it wasn't enough. In fact, I didn't have enough money for even the cheapest pair of shoes in the store. But then a woman paid the difference so I could have those shoes."

"My mom." Macey's words came out more like an exhale.

Cole nodded, remembering every detail of that day scratched into his memory. "I was so excited to have shoes that didn't need to be taped together. I showed my mom, thinking she'd be happy too."

"She wasn't?"

"Not even a little. She was so upset."

"Why's that?"

"She said we were hard workers who didn't need someone else's charity. I hadn't looked at it as charity but more about the kindness of a nice woman. But from that moment on, I felt like a charity case and vowed never to be in a position where I couldn't meet my own needs. My mom went with me and tried to return the shoes, but the young store clerk didn't know who had paid for them. She was insistent on paying back whomever had bought my shoes. My mom had a huge heart, but she also had a misguided sense of pride. I never bought that brand of shoes again."

"I'm so sorry. I can only imagine how you felt. You don't worry about the children feeling like charity cases when you donate shoes to the schools and day care centers?"

Cole shook his head. "No, because the staff puts out a letter letting parents know about the donated shoes. Those who need them can send in a signed form. The shoes are given to the children's parents at pickup or drop-off. That way, the other kids don't know who's being blessed with the shoes."

"Blessed. That's a great way to look at it. But your mom didn't take it as a blessing, I take it."

"No, she looked at it as a handout. I don't know if you know this or not, but my dad's family was very wealthy. Look at my uncle. When my dad started dating my mom, his parents claimed my mom was after my dad for his money. My mother vowed not to take a cent from them. She never applied for government food assistance, heating help, or subsidy for my care. She said if we couldn't earn it and pay for it, then we didn't need it. I guess that's why I stay in my job and don't look into government programs to help my daughter."

"But that's different, Cole. You're certainly not abusing the system. So many of the programs are in place to help children like Lexi get the best care possible, especially when some insurance programs can't meet that gap."

"I understand that, but if I can care for her on my own, then there's room for another child in those programs who can't afford basic needs like medical care. I'm not trying to be obstinate like my mom or even irresponsible. I can afford the wonderful care Lexi receives through her pediatrician without an issue. With the recent changes in her hearing though, she needs expensive hearing aids. I just need to make sure I can provide for her in the way she deserves."

"And that's why this promotion is so important to you."

"I'll be promoted to chief executive officer for the Durango area, which includes a substantial pay raise. That means I can afford the specialists Lexi needs."

"You're a good father. Don't allow your uncle to make you feel otherwise."

The timer on the oven went off. Macey slipped on silicone oven mitts that went to her elbow and pulled the first pie out of the oven. The scents of cinnamon and sugar tinged the air. Once all the pies were on the cooling racks, she removed the mitts and hung them on the peg near the oven.

"Thanks for helping me. You made the evening go by much quicker."

"Is that my cue to leave?" Cole took a step closer and brushed a dust of cinnamon off her cheek with the back of his hand.

Macey's eyes searched his face. She reached for his hand. But instead of pushing it away, she lowered it and kept her fingers wrapped around his. She shook her head. "No. I don't want you to go."

Her admission speared his gut. Then he slid his free hand over her cheek and around the curve of her neck.

Standing so close he could see the glints of gold in her brown eyes and count the number of lashes on their lids. He drew her toward him, lowered his head and kissed her.

Macey slid her arms around him.

He could taste apple and sugar on her lips.

A moment later, Cole pulled his mouth away from hers. He pressed his forehead to hers, then dropped a kiss on the tip of her nose. Then he wrapped her in his arms as she rested her cheek against his chest.

She sighed.

For a moment, he focused on the perfect way she fit into his embrace, the way her arms held him close to her.

She wanted this as much as he did, and that filled him with an emotion he couldn't quite decipher. All he wanted to do was imprint this moment into his memory.

Macey moved out of his arms. She left the room, then returned a moment later with her camera in hand. "I'm going to take a picture of you in that apron and with one of the pies. I know Aunt Lynetta would love to hang it on the wall next to your mom's picture along with her crust recipe."

He stepped forward, gently removed the camera from her hand and set it safely on the counter. Then he pulled her close once again and traced a finger along her jaw. "I told you that was a family secret. How can I buy your silence?"

Her eyes searched his. Then she stood on her tiptoes and kissed him again.

After a few moments, Cole put some necessary distance between them and moved into the dark dining room. Hands in his pockets, he stood in front of the large window and watched the snow fall lightly and drift against the lamppost that cast halos against the blanket of white.

"Cole?"

He turned at her quiet words. Macey stood in the doorway between the kitchen and the server station. The light from the kitchen turned her dark hair to gold. She held her hands in front of her, her fingers twisted together.

"You okay?"

Nodding, he ate up the distance between them in two long strides. He brushed his thumb across her cheekbone and smiled. "I'm more than okay."

She waved back toward the kitchen. "Good. When you left the kitchen, I thought…"

"What?"

"That I'd disappointed you or something."

The vulnerability on Macey's face had him swallowing the laughter at her ludicrous suggestion. "Hardly. More like the opposite. I'd like nothing more than to keep kissing."

Her arms entwined around his neck. "You should listen to your intuition."

"I would love that. More than you know, but it's nearly midnight. I think I should help you clean up and make sure you get home safely. The last thing I want is for someone to get wind of me being here and jump to the wrong conclusions."

She tugged on his apron as a grin lit up her face. "You just don't want anyone to see you wearing one of Aunt Lynetta's aprons."

He covered her hands with his own. "We're selling tickets tomorrow, but want to go together? I can pick you up. You know, so we can watch our pies take the highest bids."

"Of course. For the sake of the pies, I'd love to go with you, but I'll meet you there. No need to go out of your way."

"I don't mind going out of my way for you, Macey."

"I'll need to be there early to help set up. Text me when you arrive, and we can meet up."

"Great, it's a date."

"I like the sound of that." Macey shot him a coy smile. Then she brushed a light kiss across his lips and stepped back.

He did too.

Finally, his relationship with Macey was heading in the right direction. He'd do whatever it took to prove he was the kind of guy she could trust.

Chapter Nine

Maybe last night had been a mistake.

And that was why Cole had texted before 7:00 a.m. and apologetically bailed on her, saying he'd gotten called into work and would meet her at noon instead.

That's when he planned to meet his cousin and get Lexi. So maybe he didn't want to be alone with Macey again?

Was he regretting last night? What if he changed his mind about showing up at all?

Too many what-ifs and maybes and reliving those kisses had kept her awake until the early morning hours.

She hated the cliché of being weak in the knees, but that's how he made her feel. And she wasn't quite sure what to make of it.

Cole had texted to say he'd be there around noon, and she'd simply have to be patient. The closer the hands on her watch edged toward twelve, her stomach jumped at the thought of seeing him again.

Macey appreciated Cole's mad pie-making skills... and his company, if she was being honest. Much more than she'd expected. Especially the kisses.

Did he regret kissing her?

Maybe he didn't want to get invested in a relationship that couldn't go anywhere.

Or could it?

No, not at all.

Last night had to be a one-time thing.

She was setting herself up for heartache once again.

She needed to put last night out of her mind and enjoy herself. Having arrived at the festival before nine, Macey had stayed busy helping her mother prepare food at the pavilion and sell tickets to the Sweetheart Ball. She enjoyed walking down memory lane with friends and neighbors.

Located in the municipal park where baseball games were held during the summer, Aspen Ridge's annual WinterFest drew in tourists from surrounding areas with promises of a tubing race, an ice-carving contest, sleigh rides, and fireworks to close once the stars made their appearance. Not to mention the hot food available for sale and the traditional pie auction.

A veil of white draped over the mountains allowing the silvery-gray peaks to showcase their depths against the turquoise sky streaked with lingering clouds. Spindly and bare aspens stood among the pines laden with blankets of snow. The river cut through the edge of the park, its icy surface frosted with snow except where swimmers plunged into its frigid depths for the annual polar bear swim that raised money for the high school water sports program.

Although Macey hadn't attended in years, the festival had tripled in size, judging by her family's comments. Festivalgoers trundled from event to event dressed in colorful outerwear, heavy boots, and thick hats and scarves to protect against the single-digit temperature, and snow flurries drifting through the air.

Rounding the enormous three-sided tent someone had pitched for a makeshift barn, Macey watched a little boy dressed in a bright blue-and-red snowsuit petting a wooly lamb in a small pen. He giggled as the small animal licked his hand. Next to him, two little girls held carrots out to a couple of long-eared goats.

The scents of cotton candy and popcorn drifted from the food pavilion, reminding her of parades and summer fairs. Her stomach rumbled. She hadn't eaten anything since dragging herself out of bed to do chores before the sun had even made an appearance. And then it was a quick cup of coffee and a muffin she'd eaten on the way to the festival.

She headed toward the large pavilion in search of hot coffee, Mom's vegetable beef soup, and maybe a slice of pie. Inside, she pulled off her sunglasses and tucked them in her pocket.

Long wooden tables covered in white plastic and decorated with blue-and-white flower arrangements that would be given away to festivalgoers lined the long room. People filled most of the seats as they sought refuge from the cold or dug into the hot food being served by Mom's church.

Macey passed by the corner table she and Mom had set up showcasing Stone River Ranch and its benefits to the community. People could also purchase tickets to the ball.

Two middle-aged women dressed in white puffy jackets with faux-fur-trimmed hoods stood with their heads together, their backs to everyone else. Despite their hoarse whispers, their words trailed to Macey's ears.

"I don't understand the big deal. Crawford's asking for only a few acres. Surely they can part with some to help the community. They're being selfish, if you ask me."

"You're preaching to the choir, sister. I'd love to be able to shop at more than Regals or Sadie's. I'm tired of driving all the way to Durango to find a decent dress. And ordering online, you don't know what the quality will be. I want to feel something before I buy it."

Macey hesitated a moment before walking up behind the two women. "Hey, ladies. Can I help you with anything? Answer any questions?"

One of the women looked over her shoulder, then her eyes widened behind her round glasses. She nudged her friend. They turned and lifted their chins. "We were talking about the strip mall."

Macey schooled her tone and forced a smile. "So I heard. You know, that land has been in my family for over two hundred years. How would you feel if the government or a developer wanted to buy your house and tear it down to build a road?"

"Well, I don't know. It would have to depend on the price."

"What if the price they offered didn't match what your property was worth? Would you still go for it?"

"Absolutely not."

"I'm sure others may think my family is being selfish, but there are other considerations. The land in question belonged to my grandparents. Also, we need to be concerned with how the strip mall will affect our water system, logistics for moving cattle, and the noise and pollution from the commercial buildings."

"But what about the jobs that it will bring in? And more tourists to Aspen Ridge?"

"What about stores like Regals Shoes, Curly's Hardware and Sadie's Dress Shop? Or even Jacie's Bridal? Those bigger stores could drive these privately owned shops out of business."

"Young lady, I respect your position and all, but I still think it will be a benefit to the community, so I'm all for that."

"Will you still feel that way when your taxes increase?"

"You don't know that's going to happen."

"There are many factors at play by bringing in more commercial businesses. Aspen Ridge has prided itself on having family-owned businesses and creating a community that's safe to raise our children. The more corporate retailers we bring in, the more growth we're going to experience. Growth is good, but do you want to see Aspen Ridge becoming the size of Durango? More and more private properties like my family's and Heath Walker's will be taken from us for the 'good of the community.'"

They shrugged. Realizing she wasn't about to change their minds, Macey flashed them a bright smile. "Hope you ladies have a nice day."

With her appetite gone, Macey left the pavilion.

Was she on the right side of the fight?

Could Crawford's money make a difference at the ranch? She truly wanted to preserve her family's land, but she also wanted what was best for the community.

But no, this wasn't it. She felt it in her bones.

She refused to look at her watch, check her phone for a text from Cole, or scan the crowd to see if he'd arrived. She wasn't going to be that girl who needed a man by her side to enjoy her day.

As she rounded the corner of the makeshift barn, she nearly knocked over a child. She thrust out her hands to steady little arms covered in pink. "Oh, I'm so sorry."

The child pushed up her hat and looked up at her with tearstained reddened cheeks.

Lexi Crawford.

Macey's heart quickened as she crouched in front of the little girl. She ran a thumb over a fresh tear trailing down her rounded cheek. "Lexi, honey, what's wrong?"

"My Piper is lost." Lexi threw herself into Macey's arms and sobbed.

"Piper is lost?" She gathered the child close as she scanned the crowd around the sheep and goats.

Lexi nodded, her watery eyes wide. "I stopped to look at the sheeps. They have fluffy wool. I turned around. Piper was gone. She's lost. I just know it."

"Oh, honey, I'll help you find her. Okay?"

Nodding, Lexi rubbed her eye with a mittened fist and reached for Macey's hand.

Macey gave her a gentle squeeze. She pulled her phone out of her back pocket and tapped on her mother's number. "Hey, Mom. Have you seen Piper Healy around? I have Lexi with me. They became separated."

"No, honey, I haven't. I've been serving food for the last hour or so. Did you check in at the information booth?"

"I'll head that way. Maybe we'll cross paths with her." Macey stowed her phone. "Hey, Lexi, want to walk with me and we'll try to find Piper?"

Lexi nodded.

They walked through the crowds with Lexi gripping her hand.

"Lexi!"

Macey turned. Avery Healy ran toward them. Then she stopped, turned and waved her hand. "Mom, there she is!"

Macey pointed at Piper running toward them. "Look, Lexi. There's Piper. She's not lost, after all."

Lexi released Macey's hand and ran into Piper's outstretched arms. She cradled Lexi against her and looked at Macey over Lexi's shoulder, her eyes shimmering. "Thank you so much. I don't know what happened. One minute she was there, the next minute she was gone."

"You can't wander off like that, young lady." Lexi leaned back and shook her finger at Piper.

Piper smothered a smile and attempted a serious look. "I can't wander off?"

"No, because I was scared. I couldn't find you."

"Oh, honey. I'm so sorry I scared you. I promise not to wander off anymore."

Lexi threw her arms around Piper's neck. "Good. I missed you."

"Oh, baby, I missed you too. You have no idea. How about if we call your daddy and see when he's planning to meet us? He should've been here by now." Piper pushed back the sleeve of her jacket to look at her watch.

"Cole's meeting you around noon, right?" Macey tried to keep her tone casual.

Piper's eyebrow lifted as her lips twitched. "That was the plan. He seemed very excited about attending. Mentioned something about not wanting to miss the pie auction."

Macey's cheeks heated.

Perhaps last night wasn't a mistake after all.

She'd simply have to be patient and find out.

The morning hadn't gone as Cole had planned. But anytime Wallace was involved, that was par for the course.

Having been summoned to the job site first thing this morning, Cole wavered between telling his uncle he had plans and meeting up with Macey at a later time.

Unfortunately, his uncle won out.

Again.

Hopefully, Macey would forgive him, and he could make it up to her.

That idea kept him company as he worked through the tasks that certainly could have waited until Monday.

After last night's pie-making date—was that a date? Maybe not a scheduled one, but it sure felt like one to him. Especially the kissing.

The more he talked with Macey, the less satisfied he was with his uncle constantly barking orders at him like a drill instructor. Please and thank you weren't a part of the man's vocabulary.

Right now, he needed to focus on getting the job done so he could meet Macey. Hopefully, she wouldn't ditch him. But he wouldn't blame her if she did.

Cole grabbed his hard hat and strode from the mobile office parked behind the new condos at the end of town near the river. Head bent against the wind, he entered one of the buildings and found his foreman overseeing a wiring job in one of the unit kitchens, which was nothing more than an open room with visible studs. "Hey, Miller. How's the timeline on this project? Still on track to have the subcontractor come on Monday to install insulation and drywall?"

The foreman who had at least twenty years on Cole nodded. "Despite being down a man, we're still on track. You can notify Grady and his crew they can begin work on Monday. We'll have this finished today."

Cole clapped him on the back. "Thanks, man. Knew I could count on you."

"Maybe not for much longer though."

"Oh? What's going on?"

Miller pulled off his baseball hat and scratched the back of his balding head. "I planned to stop by the office during my lunch break to talk, but I guess now's as good a time as any. I'm turning in my two weeks' notice."

Cole swallowed the sigh pressing on his chest. "Why's that?"

"I've been offered another job with Heath Walker. After losing his ranch, he started a construction company a few months ago. He's looking for a new foreman. Less pay, but the benefits are better. At this point in my life, I need less stress. Too many long days and not enough time to see my wife and kids is taking its toll. My daughter's getting married soon, and Crawford's giving me a hard time about taking the day off. Not right, man. Not right at all."

"No, it's not. It'll be tough to see you go. You're the best foreman on my crew."

"Just so you know, it's not you. The guys and me, we like working for you. But when Crawford's on-site, well, let's just say morale goes down." He thumped his hat against his thigh before returning it to his head.

"I hear you, and I'm sorry about that."

"I shouldn't say anything with him being your uncle

and all, but he really does need some better people skills."

Cole laughed. "No joke. Listen, if there's anything I can do, let me know. You're good people, Miller, and I'll put in a word if you need me to."

"Thanks. I appreciate it."

Cole headed back to the field office trailer, tossed the clipboard on the desk, then dropped in the chair. He dragged a hand over his face and blew out the pent-up sigh.

The door flung open, and Wallace strode inside, pulling in a blast of cold air and shrinking the small room with his bulk. "Hey, I don't pay you to sit around."

Pushing to his feet, Cole gritted his teeth. "I just walked back in from the site. Looks like we need to start interviewing a new foreman."

"What's wrong with Miller?"

"He's putting in his two weeks." Cole palmed his empty cup and reached for the nearly empty coffeepot.

Wallace grabbed a clean cup off the shelf above the microwave and mini fridge. He took the pot out of Cole's hand and drained it into his own cup. "He what? No way. We have a job to finish."

Cole looked at the empty pot and shook his head. He flicked off the coffee maker and dropped his cup back on the desk. "The man's exhausted. Too many long hours with not enough time off."

"Cry me a river. The man's gone soft."

"He had a heart attack, Wallace. He came back to work sooner than the doctor wanted him to because you wouldn't stop hassling him."

"Like I said, we have a job to do."

"And it's getting done, but you really need to relax."

Crawford's head swiveled. His eyebrow raised as he took a step closer to Cole. "What'd you say?"

"You heard me." Hands curled at his sides, Cole stood firm, feet apart.

"I don't think so because it sounded like you were being pretty mouthy."

"Listen, I'm not a teenager you can bully into submission. I do my job, and I do it well." He waved a hand toward the condos. "So do they. You're coming down on them hard, but they're doing everything they can to stay on track. Ease up a little and give them some breathing space before they all walk off the job. Then where will you be?"

"I have half a mind to fire them and bring in a new crew who aren't a bunch of crybabies."

"Go for it, but you'd better plan on hiring a new project manager as well because I'll be leading the walk-off."

Wallace scoffed. "Right. Like you'll leave and risk losing your daughter's health insurance."

"You're not the only developer. I can get another job. With better pay and insurance. Plus I won't have to be a pawn in this manipulative game you're playing against the Stones."

Wallace's eyes blazed and he poked a stubby finger into Cole's chest. "Listen to me, boy, you go ahead and try. I'll see to it the only job you can get is at a fast food joint."

Cole lifted a shoulder. "Hey, that's honest work, so don't knock it."

"You owe me, and you know it."

"Actually, I don't."

The lines deepened in Wallace's forehead. "What

are you talking about? Who put you through college? Who paid for those fancy duds you wore? Who bought your first car?"

"I bought the car. You just didn't like me having a sliver of independence, so you bought me a newer one. Plus I worked two jobs to help pay for my tuition, so it's not like you wrote a check for the full amount and you know it." Cole glanced at his watch. "I told you I'd work until noon, and it's already after one. I need to pick up Lexi."

"Fine. Whatever. Be at the municipal building first thing Tuesday morning, and leave your bleeding heart at home. We're meeting with the Stones to review the appraisals and to present them our final offer. We'll be celebrating or filing a complaint with the court come lunchtime."

Without saying goodbye, Cole stalked out of the trailer and slammed the door behind him. As he headed for his car, Wallace's words ignited his anger with each step.

He pulled into the lot at the park where WinterFest was being held and looked for Macey's car but didn't see it. He tried not to let its absence get to him. He didn't blame her for leaving. He should've been more considerate and contacted her when he was going to be late.

But he was there now. More than anything, he'd wanted to spend the rest of the day with Macey and Lexi. To walk together. Laugh together. Eat junk food together. And pretend they lived in a different time. Maybe even a different place and they could be a real family.

Cole never expected to be jealous of another man resigning, but part of him longed to be leaving along with Miller. Problem was, he loved his job and managing construction crews.

He loved building houses out of blocks with his dad when he was a kid. They had talked about having a business together someday. But that had never happened.

He wandered into the park, dodging two little boys chasing after each other with snowballs ready to be launched. Their parents huddled together with hands gripping steaming to-go cups.

Someday, he'd make time for a family. Lexi would be a wonderful big sister.

Problem was, every time he imagined a wife and maybe another kid, Macey's face swam into focus.

Yeah, that was a definite problem.

One he'd have to learn how to get over.

"Daddy!"

Cole spun around at the sound of the familiar voice, then knelt one knee in the snow as he opened his arms. Lexi run into his embrace and flung her arms around his neck. "Daddy, guess what? I won a teddy bear!"

"You did? That's amazing. How did you win it?"

"Macey held me while I threw the ball really super hard. I got it in the hole and won a pink teddy bear."

"Where's your bear?"

Lexi turned and pointed to the large tree, void of any leaves. "Over there with Macey."

Cole's heart tripped as he followed his daughter's finger. He missed the moment because he'd given in to his uncle's demands instead of being with his daughter.

Macey sat on a bench with Piper and Avery. A small pink bear sat on Macey's lap. He pushed to his feet, brushed the snow off his jeans and allowed his daughter to drag him over to the women. Reaching the bench, he nodded and tried to sound nonchalant. "Hey, ladies. How's it going?"

Piper tapped her watch with a gloved finger. "Did you forget how to tell time? I expected you over an hour ago."

Heat crept up his neck. "I know. I'm sorry. Wallace was in a mood. Things took longer than expected. To top it off, we had a disagreement in the office."

She held up a hand. "Say no more. The less I hear about that man, the happier I'll be." She pushed to her feet and looked at Macey. "Thanks for keeping me company, Mace. And helping with Lexi."

"My pleasure." Handing the bear to Lexi, Macey stood and brushed off her backside. Then she looked up at Cole with those warm brown eyes. "Hey, you."

More than anything, Cole longed to pull her into his arms. He glanced over her shoulder as Piper stood up behind Macey. She winked and gave him a thumbs-up. Then Cole refocused his attention on the woman stealing his heart piece by piece. "Hey, yourself."

"I have something for you." Macey pulled a large envelope from her oversize tote bag and handed it to him. "Happy birthday."

Birthday?

His hand froze. Wait, that was today? He'd been so busy lately that he'd forgotten his birthday. But Macey had remembered.

"What's this?" He eyed her, then the envelope.

"Open it and find out." Macey wrapped her arms around her waist.

Cole turned the envelope over and reached inside. He pulled out the glossy 8 x 10 photos she'd taken of Lexi. And him.

He stared at the joy in his daughter's face as Macey had captured Lexi as she laughed.

The oversize cowboy hat she'd worn had overshadowed her eyes, but it did little to diminish the happiness on her face.

The next one showed Lexi sitting solo in the saddle as Wyatt led her down the trail with the mountains tipped in snow in the background.

And the last picture...well, that was like a gut-punch. Lexi leaned against Cole's chest and looked up at him. His arms had been wrapped around her as he dropped a kiss on her forehead.

"That one's my favorite," Macey said quietly.

He looked at her, his vision blurred. And swallowed. Hard.

Clearing his throat, Cole brushed a thumb over his left cheek. He tapped the photos against his palm. "These are..." His voice cracked. He cleared his throat again. "I mean, thanks. These are so great, Macey. I saw your camera, but I didn't even realize you were taking pictures of her. Of us."

Macey slid a hand in his and gave it a light squeeze. Then she released her hold. "I apologize for not asking permission, but no one else will see these but you."

He lowered his gaze to the pictures once again as he leafed through them, then looked at her. "No, it's fine. Really. I need to get frames for these. Lexi will love them, especially the one of her on the horse. This is one of the best gifts I've ever received. Thank you."

She lifted a shoulder and toed the ground with her boot. "I'm not a pro by any means, but I like playing around with my camera when I have time."

Cole slid a finger under her chin and lifted it. "You have talent. Don't dismiss that."

Her eyes still on his, she smiled. "Are you hungry? Want some lunch? Or maybe some birthday pie?"

As her eyebrow lifted, a spark ignited in his gut at her suggestion. "After peeling all those apples last night, I didn't think I'd want to see another one. But a warm slice of apple pie sounds perfect right now. Especially when I'm joined by my two favorite ladies."

With Lexi holding his left hand, he longed to grab Macey's with his right, but he didn't want to scare her off. Instead, he had to settle for brushing his shoulder against hers.

For now.

The moment they were alone, he planned to pull her into his arms. She'd fit so perfectly there.

She'd fit perfectly into his life as well.

Chapter Ten

How had everything gotten turned around so fast?

Less than a week ago, Macey and Cole had spent Saturday at WinterFest with Lexi, laughing, talking and having the best time.

Now, four days later, they sat on opposing sides of the courtroom.

Macey pressed a hand against her churning stomach as she tried to focus on the judge's words. He smacked his gavel, causing her to jump.

Her eyes skated across the aisle as Cole hung his head. But Wallace high-fived members of the city council.

Macey leaned forward and found Bear with his head in his hands, Wyatt shaking his head, Mom and Dad holding hands and Everly dabbing her eyes.

They had lost.

Despite the family's best efforts of trying to rally the community to get behind preserving the ranch, the judge ruled in favor of the Aspen Ridge City Council—and the strip mall.

Without looking at anyone, especially Cole, Macey

stood, walked down the aisle and pushed through the courtroom doors.

She didn't need to see Wallace Crawford gloat.

Standing in the hallway, she rubbed her chilled hands over her arms. Despite standing next to the aging radiator, the heat did little to thaw the numbness in her limbs.

Dressed in a navy skirt with matching jacket, Macey wanted nothing more than to shed the suit for her jeans and a final ride to South Bend before Crawford took possession of the land.

Outside the courtroom, walls painted the color of aged parchment held framed photos of different parts of the county. Was it a coincidence that Macey happened to stand next to the one that showcased South Bend as the original homestead?

She pressed a hand against the dark paneling lining the bottom half of the wall and tapped a toe against the polished floor tile.

The disastrous meeting on Tuesday between her family and the city council and Wallace Crawford reviewing all of the appraisers' findings ended with her father and Wallace Crawford exchanging heated words. Her father accused Crawford of trying to lowball their family, and he rejected the city council's final offer. The city council filed a petition in condemnation with the court—most likely at Crawford's urging.

Aaron Brewster had been certain it would have taken several months for the case to come before the judge, but someone pulled strings to get it added to the court docket just two days after the meeting.

And then they lost anyway.

Dad exited the courtroom talking to Aaron, his lips thinned and his jaw clenched. The young attorney's hand tightened on his briefcase. Seeing Macey, he moved to her and touched her elbow. "I'm sorry, Macey."

She lifted a shoulder. "It is what it is. We lost."

"I'll file an appeal."

"Do you think it will do any good?" She tried to keep her tone even.

"I don't know, but I'm going to do everything I can to get the judge to change his mind. We'll take it to state court if we have to."

Tears filled her eyes, but she tried to blink them away as the courtroom doors opened once again and Mom walked out with Bear, Wyatt and Everly. They wandered over to her, heads down and shoulders hunched.

Macey wrapped her arms around her mother. "I'm so sorry, Mom."

"Me, too, sweetheart. Me, too."

Wyatt stood behind Dad, feet apart and his hands clasped behind his back in a perfect military stance. His jaw tightened. Bear ran his fingers along the brim of his hat while he and Dad continued their conversation with Aaron.

Wallace Crawford strutted out of the courtroom with his legal team and members of the city council. Cole trailed behind. His eyes caught Macey's, but she forced herself to look away. He started toward her family, and she turned her shoulder away from him. Maybe he'd take the hint.

The last thing they needed to hear was a bunch of meaningless words. Especially her.

Cole had chosen his side.

And she'd have to live with that.

"Cole. Get a move on it." Wallace Crawford's bellowing voice bounced off the hallway walls.

Cole followed his uncle out the doors.

Somehow, they needed to figure out how to move past this loss. For her, it wasn't just the loss of her grandparents' legacy, but also knowing her relationship with Cole wouldn't be the same again.

She gave herself another swift mental kick for allowing him into her personal circle. For letting her defenses down. She knew better but did it anyway, thinking and hoping for a different resolution.

"Let's head to the diner. Lynetta needs to hear the news from us." Without another word, Dad slipped an arm around Mom's waist and guided her through the lobby and out the door.

Mom rested her head on his shoulder a moment. He whispered something in her ear, and she nodded. He placed a gentle kiss on her forehead.

With everything her parents had gone through, their love continued to grow.

Macey envied that.

Would she have someone who loved and supported her? Someone who stood up for her?

While Cole may be a great father and have other traits that would make him perfect husband material, they couldn't have a future together as long as he worked for his uncle.

Wyatt cupped the back of Macey's neck. "Come on, sis. Let's ditch this place. It's giving me hives."

Ten minutes later, they gathered at the diner, hands wrapped around white mugs filled with steaming coffee, but no one said anything.

The server took their order, then Dad leaned back

in his chair, his eyes weary as lines deepened in his forehead. He looked at each one of them and shook his head. "Well, aren't we a sorry bunch of sad sacks? Are we going to sit here and wallow and let Crawford steal our joy?"

"He's already gaining our land." Bear toyed with his spoon.

"While I don't agree with the man's methods, we do need to abide by the judge's ruling. For now."

"Aaron plans to appeal." Macey stirred cream into her coffee.

Bear scowled. "That could take months."

"Months that we still retain our property."

Dad leaned forward and sipped his coffee. "Listen, we haven't been beaten yet. Sure, this was a curveball, but remember—God's in control. If He wants us to keep our land, then He'll work it out. We need to trust Him. In the meantime, we keep representing the family and standing up for those values that have made us who we are today." He lifted his mug.

Even though Macey didn't have the same perspective, she lifted her mug and clinked it against the others.

Just then, the door flew open, and Lexi ran in. Cole followed her, saw Macey's family sitting at a table near the counter and reached for Lexi. He knelt in front of her and talked too low for Macey to catch his words.

She folded her arms over her chest and shook her head so hard that her braids smacked her in the cheeks. "No, Daddy. I don't wanna go. I want Netta's pancakes."

Cole's face turned the same cherry red as the vinyl on the stools lining the counter. He took his daughter's hand and started to pull her toward the booths lining the wall on the other side of the dining room.

As Lexi turned, she locked eyes with Macey. She pulled her hand out of her father's grasp and raced over to the Stones' table. She tapped a finger against her teeth. "Look, Macey. Piper took me to the dentist. He counted my teeth. No cabities."

"That's so good to hear, sweetie." Macey gathered the child in her arms and buried her face in the little girl's hair, which smelled of baby shampoo. A lump formed in her throat.

"Can I sit with you?" She looked up at Macey with the sweetest smile on her innocent face.

Macey tightened her hold around the child who had wiggled her way into her heart, and tried to find the right words. More than anything she wanted to say yes, but... "Lexi—"

"Lexi, leave Macey and her family alone." Cole strode to their table, his face still red and his jaw tight. "I'm sorry about that."

"But, Daddy, I wanna sit with Macey."

"Not today." He lifted Lexi off Macey's lap and carried the kicking child back out of the diner.

Macey lowered her head and closed her eyes to hold back the tears threatening to fall.

"Hey, you okay?" Everly placed a hand between Macey's shoulder blades.

Opening her eyes, Macey forced a smile and nodded, not quite trusting her voice. She rested her head against her sister's and let out a sigh. Needing some air, Macey stood and reached for her coat. "I'm going to take a walk. Meet you back at the ranch."

She stepped outside and pulled the lapels of her coat closer together as the cold hit her.

"Macey."

She froze and didn't turn at Cole saying her name.

"Can we talk?" The plea in his voice was nearly her undoing.

Without answering, she rounded the corner and headed for the path that snaked along the river. Spying a bench overlooking the water, she brushed off the snow and sat, the cold metal pressing into the backs of her legs.

He sat next to her. Leaning forward, he braced his elbows on his knees and clasped his hands. "I'm sorry. I know this didn't go the way you wanted. I wish I could fix it."

"Where's Lexi?"

"With Everly. I had no right, but I asked her to stay with Lexi so I could talk to you."

The cold seeped through her dress clothes, and Macey stood. Hands shoved deep in her pockets, she finally faced Cole, releasing a brittle laugh. "You're right, Cole. None of this has gone the way we'd hoped. Who wants to have their private property taken away from them?"

He stood and reached for her. She stepped back and nearly lost her footing. Stupid idea to walk a snowy path in heels.

Cole grabbed her arms and drew her close. "None of this has to change what's happening between us."

Her heart slammed against her ribs. She pressed her hands against his chest to prevent him from drawing her into his embrace. "How can you say that? My family is losing part of our property, and you work for the man who was instrumental in taking it. I really wish things were different, Cole. I really do. But we have no future as long as you're working for your uncle. I'm sorry for the lack of notice, but after this week, I feel like I can no longer care for Lexi. The more we're together, the harder it's going to be to say goodbye."

"Goodbye? We live in the same town. We're bound to run into each other."

"I need some space."

"Ugh. I hate that phrase. My ex-wife said the same thing when she walked out of my life."

"I'm not your ex-wife, Cole."

"You're nothing like her. I get that." He shoved his hands in the pockets of his overcoat. "I wish I could say I understand, but I don't." He took a step toward her and cupped her chin. He looked into her eyes, and she fought to hold his gaze. "I love you, Macey."

Hearing those four words should've sent her running into his arms. Instead, she shook her head, took a step back and held up a hand. "Please don't, Cole."

"Don't what? Feel how I feel? That's not possible." He raked a hand through his hair. "What about the Sweetheart Ball? It's in two days, and I wanted you to come with me as my date."

"I'll finish the final details by myself. But I think it would be best if we attended separately."

"We agreed to see it through to the end."

"The end. How fitting." She laughed, but there was no humor in this situation. Dropping her eyes to her frozen toes, she shook her head. "This will be the last Sweetheart Ball at South Bend. The end of an era." She lifted her head and looked at him again. "And the end of you and me. I'm sorry, Cole, but the answer is no."

The look of anguish that crossed his face nearly had her snatching back her words. But she forced herself to remain quiet. No matter how much it ached to reject his request, Cole couldn't be a part of her life.

Without another word, she headed back to the diner, tears sliding down her cheeks.

She'd give anything to book a tropical vacation somewhere to escape this mess. Perhaps a little distance would heal the ache in her chest.

Who was she kidding?

No amount of miles between them could ease the pain of a broken heart.

Cole had nothing to celebrate.

While Wallace took this as a great victory, Cole viewed it as a loss. In more ways than one.

Even though he worked for his uncle, he'd been praying for the judge to side with the Stone family. Even if it meant losing the promised promotion.

After seeing the tears in Macey's eyes, Cole felt ashamed. How could he have been a part of taking from the family who'd done nothing but give to him?

Watching Macey walk away had been one of the most painful experiences in his life. Even though he knew they could be good together, he needed to give her time.

Somehow, he needed to make it right.

But how?

"Cole, why aren't you celebrating with us?" Wallace stood in the open doorway of his office.

Cole strode out into the hall, shoving his hands in his front pocket. "You don't need me."

"Of course, I do. Without you, this wouldn't have been possible."

"You wanted me to get them to sign. They didn't sign."

"Semantics. We still got the land. That's the important thing, right?" Wallace turned away when someone from inside his office called his name.

"If you say so," Cole muttered, heading back to his office, closing the door to drown out the sounds from across the hall.

One of the drawbacks of spending so much time on the work sites was he spent only one day a week in his regular office. With court this morning, his work time was shortened. Maybe he could ask Piper to keep Lexi so he could catch up on work. But he'd asked her already to take Lexi to the dentist, and she was caring for her for the rest of the afternoon.

He needed to stop relying on his cousin so much.

Cole needed to hire a nanny.

But did he really want to get in the habit of spending more and more time at the office? He'd end up like his uncle, who was the last person Cole wanted to emulate.

As he opened his laptop to search for nannies in the area, Cole bumped a picture frame on his desk. He picked up the photo Macey had taken of him and Lexi on the horse the day they'd ridden together at Stone River.

He didn't know much about photography—he could barely take a decent picture of Lexi with his cell phone, but he did know how Macey's pictures made him feel.

The way she captured his daughter's joy and light in her eyes stole his breath. She managed to draw out Lexi's best qualities in a single photo.

She brought out his best qualities as well.

He deleted his search query. He didn't want a nanny.

He wanted Macey. And not only to care for his daughter.

He loved her. Now he needed to find a way to prove how good they could be together.

A knock sounded on his closed door, then it opened.

Bernice, Wallace's secretary, stuck her head inside, waving a manila envelope. "Hey, Cole. This just came for you."

Cole rounded his desk and took it from her "Thanks, Bernice."

After she left, Cole pulled out the contents and found a letter from Barry Harrelson, Wyatt's private investigator buddy, who Cole had met with to look into his uncle's business dealings, detailing his findings.

Included with a police report were witness statements from a pair of teens who'd been given a couple hundred bucks by his uncle to trash the Stone place. Things didn't look good for his uncle or his business.

If only this information had come yesterday. Then the Stones may have been spared the heartache of going to court. And Macey wouldn't have walked away, taking pieces of his heart with her.

Now that he had these facts, he needed to figure out the best way to handle the situation in order to protect those who mattered most to him.

Chapter Eleven

Macey wasn't sure she heard correctly.

Maybe it was lack of sleep or the pounding headache from crying into her pillow half the night, but Dad's words must not have registered.

"What do you mean you're not going to appeal?" Tightening her grip on the red scoop she used to drop grain into the feed buckets, Macey tried to keep her voice level, but the tightening in her chest caused a spike in her words.

Once the horses made their way to their stalls, Mom filled their water troughs. Dark circles shadowed her eyes, and her shoulders slumped as she leaned against Patience's stall door.

Head bent, Dad pressed his back against the closed tack room door and tipped up his dusty cowboy hat, revealing weary eyes. Deep lines bracketed his mouth. He coughed into a closed fist, a deep sound rattling from the depths of his barrel chest. "I'm tired, Mace. Your mother's tired. She deserves a vacation, and I want to take her away from this mess for a while."

"Dad, I get that. Both of you are the hardest working people I know and deserve to get away." Macey dropped the scoop in the wheelbarrow and slid an arm around Mom's shoulders, giving her a light squeeze. "But please reconsider accepting the offer. There's still hope with an appeal. And we can retain our property a little longer."

Mom slid a lock of Macey's hair that had fallen out of her ponytail behind her ear. "I know you're upset—"

"Upset is putting it mildly, Mom. South Bend is the core of who we are. Without it, we wouldn't have the rest of Stone River. Selling it feels like we're cutting away our foundation." Tears flushed her eyes. She ducked her head and reached for the broom.

"I'm well aware of what the property means to this family, Macey. Do you think I like this? None of it has sat well with me since we were served with the first notice. But there comes a time when we need to stop fighting."

Macey thrust her hands in the air. "Dad, there's a difference between fighting and giving up."

"Hey, if you want to think I'm giving up, then that's on you." Dad pushed away from the tack room door. Hands fisted, he glared at her with fire, fatigue…and maybe a little fear in his eyes. "I've spent my whole life on this ranch, and it's gutting me to see it being torn apart. But I have to think about what is best for this family."

Mom stepped between them and placed a hand on his chest. "Deacon, please calm down. You're going to start coughing again. The last thing I want is for you to end up back in the hospital."

"I am calm." His growl betrayed his words.

Mom blew hair out of her face and took the broom

from Macey. She swept spilled feed into the dustpan. Always the one to come in to clean up their messes. "There are pros and cons to accepting Wallace Crawford's offer. The money will help with improvements we need done around the ranch. And having a little extra in the bank will help during those lean months when feed prices go up and cattle prices go down."

"So if we have to sell off a little piece of our acreage for peace of mind, then so be it." Dad wrapped his arm around Mom's shoulders, the two of them facing her. A united front.

She stood alone.

Macey lowered her gaze to the toes of her barn boots, then lifted her head, her voice quiet. "But whose peace of mind, Dad? Do you really want a strip mall in your backyard? Not to mention the traffic and problems we're going to have with driving cattle."

"So we come up with a new driving plan. We adjust." Dad scraped a hand over his face. "Macey, I bleed ranch soil. I was born on this land, and I intend to die here. But in the five plus decades that I've been alive, I've seen how much work it takes to run a spread this size. The two weeks I spent in the hospital opened my eyes to a lot of things, but the greatest was how close I came to losing my life." He slapped a beefy hand against his chest. "While I'm secure in the state of my heart and know where I'll spend eternity, I'm not ready to make your mom a widow just yet. It's time I put her first and start working down her bucket list."

Macey crossed the room and grabbed on to his arm. "You can still do that, Dad. Book Mom's dream vacation. We'll all chip in and pay for it. After all, it's the least we can do when you two have given us so much."

Dad removed his hat and scratched the back of his head. "We're not taking our kids' money."

She drew in a breath and released it slowly. Schooling her tone, she looked at her father. "Will you take some advice?"

His eyes narrowed. "What's that?"

"Wait until after the Sweetheart Ball to make a decision." Oh, how she hated the pleading in her voice.

He crossed his arms over his chest, then held up a calloused finger. "On one condition."

"Name it."

"The Sweetheart Ball is tomorrow. I'll wait until Monday to announce my final decision to the family. In the meantime, I'll be praying and asking for the Lord's leading. And you have to do the same."

"Absolutely. All I want is what's best for this family." Macey flung her arms around her father's neck. "Thank you, Daddy."

He squeezed her tightly, then drew back, holding on to her elbows. He gave her a stern look, yet compassion flared in his eyes. "Even if what you want isn't what's best for the ranch?"

She considered his words, then nodding slowly. "Yes, on Monday, I'll abide by whatever decision you make. After all, the ranch is in your name, so you and Mom need to make the final decision. I just hope we don't have to watch them destroy what Grandpa and Grandma worked so hard to build."

Her phone vibrated in her back pocket. she took it out and saw Cole's face on the screen. She hesitated a moment, then her thumb hovered over the decline button.

"Talk to him."

"I have nothing to say to him."

"Then just listen."

Heaving a sigh, Macey answered. "Hello?"

"Macey. For a moment, I didn't think you were going to answer."

"For a moment, I wasn't going to."

"I'm glad you did. I need to talk to you. It's important. Will you let me escort you to the ball, then we can talk afterward?"

"I gave you my answer already, Cole. Let's not rehash this. Please."

"I'll ask one more time, and I'll respect your answer, but at least hear me out. Will you please allow me to take you to the ball and then talk afterward?"

Macey closed her eyes. Everything in her wanted to say no, end the call, and not see Cole ever again. But did she truly want to do that? After ten years of not seeing him?

Cole wasn't that teenager looking for acceptance. He was a father who adored his daughter who was put in a tough position through no fault of his own.

Could she truly blame him for that?

If she had been in his shoes, what would she have done?

"Macey?"

"I'm here. I'm thinking."

"Have you decided?"

"Okay."

"Okay...you'll go to the ball with me?"

"Yes, I'll go to the ball with you. Then we can talk. But there's still so much between us."

"Like my job."

"Well, yes, for one."

"Are you saying if I quit my job then you and I have a chance of a future together?"

"I do not want to have this discussion on the phone. Let's talk this weekend."

"I'll pick you up at seven."

"Six. I want to be there early to ensure everything's set up."

"Okay, great. Six o'clock, it is. Thank you, Macey."

She ended the call and clutched her phone in her hand.

Did she make the right choice?

Only time would tell.

It was too late to back out. No matter how much she wanted to.

But everyone expected her to show up at the Sweetheart Ball. She'd given her word, and Macey couldn't—wouldn't—let them down.

She'd put a smile in place, show up and pretend to have a great time.

The doorbell rang, and Macey's heart jumped.

Taking a final look in the mirror, she smoothed a hand over the front of her strawberry-pink A-line gown with wide straps and beaded bodice. She'd pinned her hair to the side, secured it with rhinestone combs, and curls cascaded over her left shoulder. She tucked her feet into the silver sandals she'd purchased at Regals that made her feel like Cinderella.

Hopefully, when the clock struck twelve, she wouldn't be racing away from the ball.

For the past three days, she'd been agonizing over her talk with Cole and came to the conclusion she couldn't run away because she was hurt or scared. She planned to end this evening on a high note by telling Cole she loved him.

She couldn't deny it any longer.

A light tap sounded on the door, and it opened. Her father stood in the doorway, hands tucked in his black trouser pockets. His silver-streaked hair had been combed neatly, and he looked so handsome in his black suit, white shirt, and bolo tie that used to belong to Grandpa.

He shook his head as a smile crawled across his face. "Macey, you're going to snatch that boy's breath right out of his lungs."

Macey touched one of the sprayed curls resting on her shoulder.

She could only hope.

"He's here, by the way."

"Cole?"

Dad nodded and pressed a shoulder against the door frame. "I still don't know what happened in Denver, and I know things haven't been easy since you've returned, but I'm so glad you're home. Thank you for being here for your mother and the rest of the family."

Tears warmed her eyes, and she forced them back. She didn't need to meet Cole downstairs with streaked makeup. She picked up the hem of her dress and crossed the room. "Thanks, Daddy. I'm so glad too."

He held out his elbow. "Let's not keep your young man waiting any longer."

With her stomach in knots, she took her father's elbow and they descended the steps slowly. As Cole came into view, her own breath caught in her lungs.

He stood in the foyer, a small box in one hand and his gray cowboy hat in the other. He wore a charcoal-gray suit with a tie that was nearly an exact match to the color of her dress, and polished black shoes.

As she stepped off the last step, he set his hat and the box on a nearby chair and reached for her hands, holding her at arm's length. "Wow, Macey. You look...that dress...you're beautiful."

Dad cleared his throat, and Cole dropped her hands as if he'd been stung. He straightened and cleared his throat. "Good evening, sir."

Dad nodded. "Cole."

Macey smothered a smile and retrieved her coat from the closet.

Cole took it and held it while she slipped her arms in the sleeves. He reached for his hat and handed the box to her. "I got you something."

She opened it and found a white calla lily with a bright pink center resting between two miniature white roses and greenery. She lifted the corsage to her nose. "Thank you, Cole. It's beautiful. I'll have you put it on me once we arrive at the ball, so it doesn't get flattened by my coat."

He rested a hand on the small of her back. "Ready to go?"

Was she?

She reached for her matching clutch and nodded. "I want to ensure everything is set up. I don't want anything to spoil this evening."

Cole guided Macey outside and down the cleared steps. He unlocked a silver SUV, opened the passenger door and helped her inside. He rounded the front and slid behind the wheel.

"Did you trade in your truck?"

"No, this is Piper's. She said you'd have an easier time getting into her car than my truck."

"She's not going?"

Cole started the engine. "No, she hasn't dated since Ryland died and didn't want to attend alone. She's keeping Lexi overnight. They're having a sleepover in the living room."

"Sounds like fun." Macey pressed a hand against her stomach. Why was she so nervous? She'd known Cole most of her life. The ball was set on her family's property. She knew most of the people planning to attend.

But tonight was different.

Cole headed toward South Bend and parked in front of the barn.

Light flakes of snow drifted from the inky black sky as he reached for her hand and escorted her inside.

Her breath caught. She pressed a manicured hand against her throat.

After Everly learned about her walking away from Cole, she took over decorating duties. And Macey didn't protest. She couldn't find the energy to do it on her own. Instead, she'd sent Everly her notes. She and her friends promised to make Macey proud.

And boy, did they.

How they'd manage to transform a very old barn into a fairy-tale setting escaped her. Tiny lights had been strung through yards of tulle and hung from the barn beams over long tables covered in white linens.

LED votive candles flickered at each place setting, sending light over the individual roses placed across the gleaming white plates. Bouquets of miniature pink roses, bright pink Stargazer lilies, white gerbera daisies and greenery lined the tables. The scents of the flowers fragranced the air. A stage had been set up toward the back of the barn along with an area cleared for dancing.

Uncle Pete's servers finished setting the tables and started setting out the hors d'oeuvres.

Behind her, Cole rested his hands on her shoulders. He whispered in her ear, "You did it, Mace. You pulled it off, and the place looks incredible."

She turned around, and his hands slid down her arms until he entwined his fingers with hers. She gave his hands a gentle squeeze. "Actually, Everly did the decorating."

"With your vision. This is everything we discussed, including the single roses."

"Okay, then, *we* did it together." Standing on tiptoe, she pressed a light kiss against his cheek. "Thank you for helping my family with this."

He wrapped his arms around her and held her close for a moment. "I did this for you. I think we make a great team, and I don't want it to end. It could be the beginning of something wonderful."

She longed to stay in his embrace, but it wasn't the time. For now, they needed to focus on hosting a wonderful evening.

Later, they'd talk. And it gave her one more thing to look forward to.

Chapter Twelve

Nothing would ruin tonight.

Cole planned to make sure of it.

From the moment he watched Macey walk down the steps at her parents' house, he knew, now more than ever, they were meant to be together.

Not because she looked so incredible in her dress. But it was the look in her eyes that mirrored what he was feeling in his heart.

And he couldn't wait to tell her.

Again.

But this time, he hoped she'd reciprocate those feelings.

For now, he'd mingle, enjoy dinner and stand by Macey's side as they oversaw this event that meant so much to both of them.

Cole filled two cups with punch. Then he came face-to-face with Barrett. "Hey, Bear. Good to see you, man."

Macey's brother stuffed his hands in his pockets and gave Cole a quick nod. "If it weren't for the fact that my grandparents started this annual event, I'd be holed up in my cabin watching a hockey game."

"It's good to dress up and get out every once in a while."

Bear lifted a shoulder. "If you say so. Personally, I prefer solitude over a lot of unnecessary noise." He looked around the room. "Piper didn't come?"

Cole shook his head. "She wasn't sure about getting a sitter for Avery, so she offered to watch Lexi for me."

Bear's jaw tightened. He nodded again.

Even though Cole's excuse sounded flimsy, they both knew the real reason she stayed away.

Barrett Stone.

But that was for the two of them to work out themselves. Cole wasn't about to get into the middle of that fight.

Macey joined them and slid her hand in the crook of her brother's elbow. "You clean up quite nicely, Bear. So, it is possible to wear something other than worn Levi's, your cowboy hat and still survive."

Bear smiled. Just barely. "Believe me, once dinner is over and Mom and Dad make their speech, I'm out of here. Then the suit can hang in the closet for another year."

"I'm glad you're here now." She gave him a quick hug, then turned to Cole. "Are one of those cups for me?"

Cole handed her one. "Sorry, I got sidetracked."

Moments later, they were joined by Macey's parents. Dressed in a long-sleeved red lacy gown, Mrs. Stone looked gorgeous and gave Cole an idea of how Macey could look in a couple of decades. Mr. Stone couldn't keep his eyes off his wife.

That was the kind of relationship Cole wanted.

"Macey and Cole, you two have done an incredible

job. We can't thank you enough for pitching in to make this ball happen."

Macey tucked her arm into Cole's elbow. "I couldn't have done it without Cole's help."

Cole shrugged. "I didn't do much. This is mostly Macey's doing."

She nudged him. "You did more than that and you know it, Mr. Modest. The roses were Cole's idea. And to be honest, they were a huge hit. Plus the bouquets on the tables are in memory of loved ones who lost their fights due to cardiac issues."

Mrs. Stone glanced at her husband who nodded, then she reached for Cole's hand. "We loved your mother. Losing her so young was tragic. Deacon and I have been talking, and we would like to set up a foundation in her name to help women—single mothers, especially—to ensure they have access to quality medical care. With your permission we would like to call it the Jane Crawford Heart to Heart Foundation. We'll meet with our lawyer to set up the proper paperwork. Then we'll send out the information to all of our donors so they can invest too."

Cole blinked through a sudden haze and struggled to swallow past the boulder in his throat. He brushed a thumb under his eye. "Why would you do that? After everything my uncle has done to hurt your family, and my part in trying to acquire your land?"

Mr. Stone shoved a hand in his front pocket. "One doesn't have anything to do with the other. Your mother was an important part of your life and ours. She was a hard worker who deserved more than what she got, but she never complained. All she wanted was to give you the best life. And this is one way that we can honor her. If you agree, then we will announce it tonight after dinner, son."

Son.

When Mr. Stone said it, Cole felt a sense of pride, like he was accepted and belonged. Unlike the way it felt when his uncle used it.

Cole nodded and held out his hand. "Yes, absolutely. Thank you, sir. I'm so honored. And you know my mother would be appalled by such attention."

They laughed, and Lynetta came up to them, dressed in a lovely black gown covered in some sort of silver sparkle. "Hey, guys, what do you say we find our seats so they can start serving dinner?"

"Good idea. I was too nervous to eat lunch, but now I'm famished." Instead of following her family to their table, Macey tugged on Cole's hand. "Will you come with me as I say grace?"

"You sure?"

"Yes. More than anything." The way she looked at him made Cole want to kiss her in front of everyone but he wouldn't embarrass her that way, especially not knowing how she truly felt about him.

Holding on to her hand, Cole guided her to the stage.

Macy stepped up to the microphone. "Excuse me. If everyone could find their seats, then we'll say grace and get dinner started."

Chairs scraped across the wooden floor as people settled in their places. Once the room quieted, Macey bowed her head and clasped her hands in front of her, "Dear Lord, thank You for the abundant blessings You've given each one of us. Thank You for this time we can gather together and raise money for such a worthy cause. Thank You for the food and all the hands that made this night a success. Be with those who are supporting loved ones with cardiac issues and those who have lost those they've loved. May we always remember and not take our health for granted. May the fellowship be sweet and the donations plenty. Amen."

Amens echoed throughout the barn.

Her words of thanks and gratitude flowed over him, especially the touching way she included the families who struggled with the loss of their loved ones.

He held her chair as she sat with her family, and he took his place between Macey and her aunt.

Lynetta covered his hand and gave it a gentle squeeze. "Your mom would be so proud of you."

Fresh tears washed his eyes, and he blinked them back. He hoped so.

Throughout dinner, Cole tried to pay attention to the conversation and the delicious salmon in front of him, but his focus was shaken by Macey's arm constantly brushing against his sleeve and the fragrance wafting from her hair.

As their meal progressed and their plates cleared, an assortment of desserts was delivered to each of the tables.

Cole chose flourless chocolate cake. He'd just dug his fork into the cake for his first bite when the side door flew open and slammed against the wall.

A sudden draft blew through the room.

Cole looked up from his dessert and his stomach took a nosedive.

His uncle stood in the doorway, feet apart and hands on his hips. "Well, well, well. What have we here?"

The room fell silent as Wallace strode across the floor, his footsteps measured and heavy. Mr. Stone,

Bear and Wyatt slid back their chairs and pushed to their feet.

Setting his napkin next to his plate, Cole stood and glanced at Macey. "Excuse me."

He made his way through the guests and reached Wallace. "What are you doing here?"

"It's a public event. I can be here."

"Not without a ticket. And you didn't buy one."

Wallace waved his hands. "Buy one? Why should I when this place is going to be mine soon enough? And you know what my first plan will be? I'm going to tear this eyesore down board by board."

Cole pressed a hand to his uncle's shoulder and turned him toward the door. "You need to leave."

Wallace shrugged off his hand. "Get your hands off me, boy. I'm not going anywhere."

"Yes, you are," Mr. Stone said. "Wallace, this is between you and me. If you want to settle this now, then let's step outside. But you will not ruin this event." He moved next to Cole, his voice steady and quiet.

Wallace framed his fingers around his belt buckle. "Deacon Stone, you think you're better than everyone else, but you're nothing more than a poor rancher trying to hold on to mommy and daddy's legacy."

Jaw tight, Mr. Stone took another step toward Wallace. "As I said, this is between you and me."

Someone touched Cole's sleeve. He turned and found Macey standing next to him. She reached for his hand and gave it a light squeeze.

Noticing Macey, Wallace sneered and pointed the finger at her. "And you. You come home and stir up all kinds of trouble. You say you're fighting for your family. But you're just being selfish. The strip mall would've provided jobs for the community. But you don't care about that. You're nothing more than a spoiled princess who gets whatever she wants."

Macey's cheeks reddened as Wallace's words echoed off the rafters.

Before Cole could say anything, Mr. Stone stepped between them. "Crawford, that's enough. I will not allow you to speak to my daughter like that."

Wallace moved in front of Cole and poked him in the chest. "After everything I've done for you, this is how you betray me?" He circled his finger around the Stones. "For them? You had me investigated. I can't work with people I don't trust. Now I know where your loyalties lie. Once a charity case, always a charity case. Good riddance. You can try to side with them, but face it, you don't belong."

Bear and Wyatt each grabbed one of Wallace's arms and propelled him toward the door. "It's time for you to say good night, Mr. Crawford."

"This isn't over, Cole. You can count on it," Wallace yelled over his shoulder as the Stone brothers forced him outside.

Hands deep in his pockets and shoulders hunched, Cole dropped his head as Wallace's words echoed through his head. Heat scalded his neck and crawled across his cheeks.

Who was he kidding? He didn't belong here any more than his uncle did. When people talked about tonight, they wouldn't remember all of Macey's hard work. Instead, they'd gossip about his uncle crashing the event and the venomous words he spewed.

"Is it true?"

Cole's head jerked up. Macey stood in front of him, hands clasped and eyes wide and hollow.

"Is what true?"

"Did you have your uncle investigated?"

"Yes."

"When?"

"Soon after the vandalism incident."

"You had doubts about your uncle and you didn't come forward? That kind of information could have halted the proceedings. Or at the very least, it could have given the judge a reason to wait instead of ruling in favor of the city council."

Cole held up a hand. "Macey, let me explain."

She shook her head, her eyes glistening as she bit her lips. "I think you should go."

"Go?" Surely, she didn't mean…

"Yes, go." She folded her arms over her chest. "When your uncle said all those things about me, you didn't say a word in my defense."

A decade-old memory resurfaced, and Cole heaved a sigh. "Macey, it's not like that. Your dad spoke up before I could. Everything happened so quickly. Then your brothers were hauling him to the door. I wasn't going to add to the scene by chasing after them. The investigation was one of the things I wanted to talk to you about after the ball. I just got the reports."

Macey nodded, but the skepticism on her face showed she didn't believe him. "I wish you would have confided in me about your doubts. Something, anything, to give me a little hope. But you stayed quiet. I truly thought I meant more to you than that." Macey gave him a look that splintered his heart and walked back to the table where her family sat.

A place where he didn't belong.

Pulling his keys from his pocket, Cole moved to the coat rack, grabbed his coat and hat then headed outside into the frigid February night.

The wind stung his face, but the pain was nothing compared to the shredding of his heart.

Wallace was right—he'd always be a charity case who didn't belong. Especially with someone like Macey. Somehow, he needed to figure out how to live without her.

It wasn't supposed to end like this.

Maybe he should've gone home and waited until Monday instead of going straight to the office after leaving Macey behind at the ball. Packing up his things at midnight may not have been the smartest thing to do.

At least, his uncle wouldn't have time to manipulate him into staying. It was better this way.

Still dressed in his suit but with his tie wadded up in his jacket pocket, Cole's head pounded as he shoved the rest of his personal things in his backpack. He placed the framed photo Macey had taken of Lexi on top, careful not to break the glass.

"So that's it then? After everything I've done for you? You're walking away?" Wallace fisted his hands on his hips and glared at Cole from the open doorway.

"Walking away? You just fired me, remember?"

"What was I supposed to do? You had me investigated."

"If you had nothing to hide, then what's the big deal?" Cole zipped his bag closed.

"You should've been man enough to come to me."

"I tried. You wouldn't listen and acted clueless when

I asked about my hat. I'm not taking the blame for your dirty work. If you want the Stone River property so badly, then obtain it legally."

"Oh, I have it already. Don't you remember the judge ruling in my favor?"

"Right, then you won't need me anymore." Cole slid the strap of his backpack onto his shoulder, gave his desk another glance to ensure he didn't miss anything. "Don't be surprised if the police show up with questions. The Stones' legal team will be insisting on another appraisal once they get wind of you bribing Montrose. Since their appraiser assessed their land higher than the price you offered anyway... I mean, the council offered, they may have a different opinion about fair market value."

Wallace's eyes narrowed. "You're worthless, you know that?"

Cole tried to shrug off the barb. "So you've said at least three times already. Insulting me won't help your cause, nor does it make me want to keep this job any longer."

"You wouldn't have measured up in that promotion anyway. Glad I saved myself the trouble by letting you walk now. Since the condo was another perk of working for me, consider this your eviction notice since I own that too."

"Perk? I paid rent, so I'm entitled to thirty days' notice."

He waved away Cole's words. "Whatever. You'll never be anything more than the charity case I picked up the day after your mother's funeral."

Cole fisted his hand and forced himself not to punch his uncle's smug face. "I'd rather be a charity case and have my values rather than all the money in the world and do people dirty in business."

"That goes to show how little you know about how business gets done. Everyone gets their hands dirty."

"Not me." He headed for the door. "I suggest backing out of the Stone River deal and leave the property to who it belongs."

"And I suggest you take your opinions elsewhere because no one here is listening."

"I'm sure the sheriff will listen when I talk to him about the two guys you hired to vandalize the Stones' property." Cole pulled out his keys, removed the ones to this office building and the mobile office at the Riverside Condos job site, and tossed them on his former desk.

Wallace scoffed. "No one's going to believe you."

Cole patted his computer bag and smiled. "We'll see about that."

Chuckling, Wallace shook his head. "You hypocrite. You talk about me doing dirty business, but you're doing the same thing by hiring some punk PI."

"I'm doing what's right." With that, Cole exited the office, allowing the door to slam closed behind him.

The weight of his actions slowed his steps as he crossed the parking lot to his truck. He dropped the backpack inside, then climbed in, and gripped the steering wheel as his chest tightened.

How could he provide for his daughter without a job? Or provide her with the quality medical care she deserved? And now he needed to find a new place to live. His savings would cover them for only a couple of months while he searched.

Standing up for what he believed came with a price,

and he was about to pay it. He blew out a breath, loosened his grip on the steering wheel and started the engine, trying not to dwell on the fact that his life was falling apart.

Chapter Thirteen

Macey should've woken up with a smile on her face, reliving a magical night at the Sweetheart Ball. Except when the clock struck midnight, she was home alone, tossing and turning while replaying her conversation with Cole.

Why had she reacted that way? Why couldn't she just trust him?

With a pounding headache, she forced herself out of bed and dressed quietly in her barn clothes so she didn't wake Everly.

Even though every part of her wanted nothing more than to crawl under the covers, it would've been a waste of time. She'd lain there replaying last night's events over again in her head and calling herself a fool for pushing Cole away.

He didn't deserve to be treated like that by his uncle. Or by her.

Instead of giving him a chance to explain, she insisted he leave because of her own selfishness.

Skipping the kitchen and the coffee her body was begging for, Macey headed for the mudroom and slid her feet into her boots. Then she shrugged on her barn coat and jammed a hat over her ears. Instead of jumping in the truck or grabbing one of the utility vehicles, Macey trudged through the dark, her snow-covered dirt path illuminated only by the glow of the moon. The crisp air pushed away her headache and shook her out of her fatigued haze.

As she pushed open the barn door, she was surprised to see a light on inside. Who else was up this early? Probably Bear. He seldom slept. The horses whinnied.

Macey headed upstairs to where the bales had been stacked and dropped hay through the floor door. Then she returned downstairs, broke it up and dropped hay in each of the stalls. While the horses ate, she prepared the grain specific for each one, carried the buckets to the right stalls and poured it into their feeders. Then she rinsed out their water buckets and refilled them with fresh water.

The door opened, sending shards of daylight across the barn floor. Mom stepped inside and closed it quickly to keep the cold out.

"You're up early." Cheeks red, she pulled off her hat, peeled off her gloves and stuffed them in her pocket.

"Couldn't sleep so I decided to get a start on chores. When I came in, the light was on but no one was here." Macey walked the line of stalls and peeked inside to make sure each of the horses were eating.

"Maybe Bear's up and about doing something. You know that boy hasn't slept well since his friend was killed."

"He blames himself for Ryland getting on that bull."

"Well, he shouldn't. It was an accident." Mom rounded up the buckets Macey had used and rinsed them with the hose. "Once they're done eating, I'll help you turn them out and we can get their stalls cleaned before church."

"You don't have to do that. I'll handle it. I'm staying home today." Macey grabbed a broom and swept up the leftover hay.

"You okay?"

That was a loaded question.

Macey shrugged. "I didn't sleep well. And to be honest, I don't want to face people after last night's debacle."

Mom frowned. "What are you talking about? Last night was fantastic. Sure, Wallace's outburst was uncalled for and I was disappointed when Cole left, but everything else was perfect. In fact, I think you should consider taking over the ball from now on."

Macey leaned on her broom. "You can't be serious?"

"Yes, I am." Mom put the buckets back in place and moved the hose out of the way. "You need to reframe your thinking. Last night's ball raised more money than the previous year."

"But people won't remember that. They'll be talking about Wallace's behavior."

"Let them talk, Macey. Have the courage and confidence to be above that." Mom dried her hands on her jeans, then placed them on her hips. "Just why did Cole leave early last night?"

"We had a disagreement."

"About what?" Mom's gentle tone lacked judgment.

"When his uncle said those terrible things, he didn't stand up for me. It felt like prom night all over again. But I'm not that eighteen-year-old girl anymore." Tears warmed Macey's eyes. "In the heat of the moment, though, I cared only about myself and the property. Not his feelings, or the horrible things his uncle said to him. I feel terrible and couldn't sleep because of it."

"So go apologize and make things right."

"It's not that easy."

"It doesn't have to be complicated, honey. Holding on to someone you love is more important than holding on to a piece of property." Mom hooked her elbow around Macey's. "Come on. Let's head back to the house and get breakfast going. Your dad or one of the boys can turn out the horses."

Heads ducked against the wind that howled across the pasture, they hurried down the rutted path and inside the ranch house where the warmth thawed their freezing cheeks.

The scent of fresh coffee lingered in the air.

Macey toed off her boots, hung up her coat and headed to the kitchen. The rest of the family had made it out of bed. Dad had his Bible open on the table while Tanner and Mia sat in their booster seats, eating pancakes and scrambled eggs. Everly, Bear and Wyatt sat at the breakfast bar drinking coffee while scrolling on their phones.

Dad looked up from his reading. "Macey. I expected you to still be asleep after last night."

She grabbed a cup out of the cabinet and filled it with coffee. Then she added creamer and wrapped her hands around the warm ceramic. "I tossed and turned most of the night, so I decided to start chores early. Horses need to be turned out."

Bear drained his cup and pushed back his chair. "I'll do it. I'm heading that way anyway."

He opened the dishwasher, placed his dirty dishes instead, then bumped the door closed with his hip.

The landline rang. His back to the family, Bear grabbed it. "Stone River Ranch. Barrett Stone speaking."

He listened a moment, then turned. His eyes sparked as a smile spread across his face. "You don't say. Well, thanks a lot, man. Yes, I'll let them know. Dad can give you a call tomorrow and set up a time to work out the details."

He returned the handset to the base and let out a low laugh, shaking his head. "Well, it looks like we're gonna have to tighten our belts another notch to get the money we need for improvements around here."

Dad leaned back in his chair. "Why? What's going on?"

Bear nodded toward the phone. "That was Aaron Brewster. He just had an unexpected phone call from Cole, who has proof that his uncle was behind the vandalism and paid off his appraiser to assess the land for less than what it's actually worth. On Monday, Aaron's filing a motion to stop the proceedings. The matter's been turned over to the police department. Aaron's quite sure the land will be staying in the family."

Wyatt thrust his arms in the air and let out a whoop.

Mom rounded the table and Dad hugged her so tightly he lifted her off the floor. "Cole is such a blessing. He trusted his gut and made a difficult choice. Without him, Wallace would continue to get away with his dirty tricks."

Macey stared into her coffee cup through a sheen of tears.

Once again, Dad was right—if God wanted them

to keep the land, then He'd work it out. And He used Cole to do it.

Macey needed to make this right. Not because they may be able to retain their land but because—as Mom said—it was more important holding on to someone you loved than a piece of property.

A simple apology and a request for a do-over were necessary to heal this rift between them.

Could she persuade Cole to give her another chance?

If this wasn't rock bottom, then Cole didn't know just how much harder he could hit.

The anxiety of the day twisted his gut. Somehow, he needed to get the shaking in his fingers to stop.

At least he'd done the right thing calling Aaron. He could've waited until Monday, but it seemed important to let the Stones know as soon as possible.

He stood in front of the sliding doors that overlooked his deck and stared at the river flowing behind the condo. The overhead afternoon sunshine glazed the surface, turning it frosty white. Bundled against the cold, a man, woman and small child walked a dog along the paved walkway parallel to the river.

A family.

He had the perfect child. Now he just needed the perfect wife to complete him.

Macey.

But that was out of the question now.

Every time he thought about her, an ache gripped him, making it tough to breathe.

He moved away from the doors and returned to the kitchen where an open box sat on the counter next to the sink.

He hated packing. Seemed as if half his life was spent putting everything he owned into boxes and storing it until he found his forever home.

When would that happen?

He wasn't about to uproot Lexi every couple of years when the landlord decided to raise the rent and they needed to find a cheaper place to live. It was time to buy a house, but to do that, he needed a job.

A quiet knock sounded on the front door.

Macey?

Heart in his throat, Cole hurried to open it.

He found Lynetta on the front porch, holding on to a large bag, and he forced back his disappointment. "Hey, Lynetta. Come on in."

She stepped inside, sat the bag on the floor and unwound her scarf. "You weren't in church this morning. So I wanted to stop by and check on you. How are you doing?"

"I'm fine." The automatic response slipped out before he had time to check his words.

Lynetta cocked her head, raised an eyebrow and gave him a look that said she didn't believe a word he'd said. "Cole."

He stuffed his hands in his pockets and shook his head slowly. Pressure mounted behind his eyes as weight pressed against his chest. His nose burned as his throat thickened. To his horror, tears leaked out and slid down his face, but he didn't have the strength to swipe them away.

Without a word, Lynetta wrapped him in her arms. He buried his face in her neck and wept as a tangle of fear and frustration that he'd been trying to keep knotted unraveled at her simple question. He gently separated himself from her embrace and dragged the back of his hand across his eyes.

"Sorry."

"Oh, honey, you have nothing to apologize for." She cupped his face and brushed her thumbs over his cheeks.

He waved for her to have a seat on the couch. "I didn't mean to break down like that."

"You needed to get it out." She reached for her bag and carried it into the kitchen where she unloaded several takeout boxes. "I made you a meal. And of course, pancakes for Lexi." She looked around. "Where is she, by the way? And Polly."

"They're at Piper's. After last night, I needed some time alone to think. And make a plan."

Lynetta pressed her back against the sink and folded her arms over her chest. "A plan? For what? Talk to me."

Cole rubbed his forehead, hoping to ease the throbbing behind his eyes. "I lost my job, which also includes benefits for Lexi. And since my uncle owns the condo, I need to find a new place to live. Without an income and an address, I could lose my daughter." His voice broke at that last word.

Lynetta moved over to him and cupped her hands around his face. "Listen to me—you will not lose your daughter. Before your mama died, I promised to take care of you, but then your uncle took you in. For years I carried the guilt of letting her down. I can help you now though. Pete and I have money set aside. It's yours. For whatever you need. Medical bills. Food. Start-up cost for a new apartment."

"You'll never be anything more than the charity case."

Heat crawled up his neck. He couldn't risk looking

at her, seeing the pity soaking her eyes. Cole moved out of her hands. "No, I won't take your money."

"Why not?"

"My mother taught me we are not charity cases. I need to be able to provide for my daughter on my own."

"For as much as I loved your mother, she was more stubborn than the bulls Pete used to ride. She spent most of her life proving to your father's family that she didn't need any of their money and her attitude went in the wrong direction."

"But it's up to me to make my own way. To carry my own burdens. To take care of my own problems. I can't afford to rely on the help of others. I had to rely on my uncle and he held it against me, saying I owed him. I won't owe anyone else again."

Lynetta tugged on Cole's arm, forcing him to look at her. Her brown eyes shimmered in the dim light and compassion lined her face. "Oh, honey, I am nothing like your uncle. I love you as if you were my own son. And Lexi is like the granddaughter I'll never have. There's nothing I wouldn't do in this world to protect either one of you. I love you guys."

"We love you too."

"Besides, there's a difference between being a charity case and helping someone in need. You say you have to carry your own burdens, but that's where you're wrong. Jesus died on the cross so we could lay our burdens at His feet. Burdens we weren't meant to carry, might I add. Trust God to do what He knows is best for you. And for Lexi."

Cole allowed Lynetta's words to settle into his bones. He rubbed his palms together, then dropped his hands to his side. "I don't even know where to begin. I just want what's best for my daughter."

Lynetta sandwiched his hands between hers. "There are programs in place to help you with Lexi's care. It does not make you a charity case. There's a small apartment above the diner. Our current tenant just closed on his house, and he's moving out this weekend. I'll go through and give it a good scrub, then you and Lexi can live there rent free until you can find another job."

Cole couldn't talk past the lump clogging his throat once again. "I don't know what to say."

"Say thank you." She opened her arms.

He walked into her embrace. "Thank you, Lynetta."

As he buried his face into the curve of her neck and breathed in the familiar scents of fresh-baked bread and vanilla, the burdens that had been building inside him crumbled.

Maybe by trusting and leaning into God and others, he didn't have to make his own way. Maybe he could finally lower his arms and stop carrying the world on his shoulders.

Cole taped the lid shut and wrote Dishes—Fragile on the box in black permanent marker. Then, he stacked it by the door, grabbed an empty box and headed back to the kitchen.

Inspired after talking with Lynetta, he wanted to get everything packed and be done with the condo, his uncle...all of it.

The doorbell rang in the too-quiet condo. With Lexi napping in her bed, he tried to stay quiet so he didn't disturb her.

He dropped the box by the sink and headed for the

door. He opened it to find Wyatt standing on his front porch. "Hey, man. Come in." He stepped aside to let his friend enter. "What's going on?"

He eyed the boxes. "Moving?"

"Yeah, I guess I am." Cole waved a hand toward the couch. "Have a seat. Want some coffee? I haven't packed the mugs or coffee maker yet."

"Sure, sounds good."

He headed to the kitchen and opened the cabinet. Instead of sitting on the couch, Wyatt followed him and leaned against the doorjamb. "Everything okay?"

Cole's fingers tightened around the coffeepot handle. "I'm…hanging in there."

"Anything I can do?" Wyatt took the cup Cole held out to him. "I understand hanging in there."

Instead of refilling his own mug, Cole gripped the edge of the sink. "After the fiasco at the ball, I lost my job. I'm moving above the diner until I can find a job and a house to buy. Trying not to feel like a failure."

The cup clinked against the counter as Wyatt set his coffee down. He moved beside Cole and clapped a hand on his shoulder. "I get it, man. When I lost Linnea and had to take care of Mia on my own, I felt like I was drowning without even being near a body of water."

Cole nodded, not having words to equate to the pressure that had been steadily building behind his rib cage. "How'd you survive?"

"My daughter needed a father. And I needed help. So I left the corps and returned to Stone River where my family rallied together to lend a hand."

"Yeah, I don't have that option."

"You're wrong. Even though your parents are gone,

you do have family. You have Piper. You have Lynetta. You have us."

Cole eyed him. "You guys? Right. I'm sure your family hates me after everything my uncle put them through."

"Again, you're wrong. My family loves you and always will."

"I doubt your sister shares that same sentiment."

"Macey…" Wyatt trailed off, then turned, pressed his back against the counter and folded his arms over his chest. "Well, I think you and my sister need to have a talk. To clear the air once and for all." Wyatt reached into his back pocket and pulled out his wallet. He removed a business card and handed it to Cole. "Also, if it weren't for the guys in my support group, I seriously don't know what I would've done. My family helps to lighten my load, and these guys keep me grounded. They've been there and get what I'm going through. I think they could do the same for you too. Next get-together's tomorrow night at the church. You're welcome to join us."

"I've carried everything so long on my own. I'm not sure I know how to unload onto someone else."

"Dude, I hear you. Losing my wife nearly killed me. We'd been together since ninth grade. My daughter was my saving grace. She gave me purpose, a reason to wake up each day and take that first step. When I returned to the ranch, Aunt Lynetta said to me, 'Wyatt, trusting God requires action. You need to let go of your fears and worries, then lay them at the Father's feet. Then you have to step back and allow Him to do good work, within you and for you. Yes, sometimes that requires pain, but that pain refines our faith. Take that first step.'"

Cole chuckled. "She said essentially the same thing when she dropped by earlier."

"She's a great lady. She said she wasn't meant to have her own babies so she'll take care of those around her. And she does a great job."

"She's been like a mother to me and a grandmother to Lexi."

Wyatt poked Cole's chest. "Let her in, man. Let her help. It blesses her as much as it blesses you."

Cole nodded, his throat tight. "So I'm learning."

Wyatt grinned. "The door's open. You decide if you're going to walk in."

Cole fingered the card and tapped it against his palm. "Thanks, man."

Wyatt glanced at his watch. "Oh, hey, I gotta split. I'm meeting Mom and Dad at Aaron Brewster's office. Thanks for that, by the way. It took guts."

Cole lifted a shoulder. "It was the least I could do after the pain I caused."

"Your uncle. Not you. Remember that. By the way, Macey's at the ranch looking after Tanner and Mia right now."

Cole closed the door behind Wyatt and pulled out his phone. As much as he wanted to call Macey, what could he say? He had nothing to offer her except his heart.

Would it be enough?

Chapter Fourteen

Macey couldn't deny it any longer—she missed Cole. And Lexi.

In the short time she'd been back in Aspen Ridge, they managed to become important parts of her life. She hadn't seen them in nearly a week, and a part of her felt incomplete.

She needed to stop being a chicken and apologize.

Now that the storm had passed and the sun brightened the sky on an unseasonably warm day, Macey decided to take Cheyenne out for a ride.

She wavered with texting Cole and asking him to meet her at South Bend.

What if he ignored it? Or worse, said no?

Only one way to find out, and she had to try at least.

She sat on Cheyenne and framed the waterfall through the viewfinder and manually adjusted the focus. She pressed the shutter release button and captured several images of the breaktaking landscape.

Sunshine glazed the frozen ice-blue water surrounded by craggy rocks. Above her, pine branches laden with snow bowed, creating a winter wonderland canopy. Jagged chunks of ice floated where the sun warmed the stream's surface.

Macey nudged Cheyenne forward, then dismounted. She looped horse's reins over a low-hanging branch and edged closer to the stream, balancing on the snowbank.

Stooping low to the ground, she angled her camera to shoot up the waterfall from ground level, hoping to capture the sun's rays kaleidoscoping through the crown of branches.

Cheyenne nickered and raised her head. Macey pushed to her feet and brushed snow off her legs. She turned to see what caused Cheyenne's response.

Her heart slammed against her ribs.

He came.

Raising her camera, she cupped the lens in her left hand as she focused on Cole riding Wyatt's horse, Dante. She snapped several shots of the horse kicking up snow as they drew closer.

How she managed to hold on to her camera, she didn't know. Her heart beat a steady rhythm as her nerves thrummed through her body. He'd either be happy to see her or turn the horse around and race away.

Pulling on Dante's reins, Cole slowed the stallion, then dismounted. He looped the reins around the same branch as Cheyenne's. Dante nuzzled Cheyenne, and Macey snapped a picture of the two.

Cole's dark sunglasses shaded his eyes, so Macey wasn't privy to his expression, but the slight smile on his lips caused her shoulders to relax. Dressed in jeans, boots and a charcoal-colored winter coat, he stuffed a hand in his front pocket as he ambled toward her.

She resisted smoothing down the tangles from the

wind dancing through her hair. "Hey. I wasn't so sure you'd come."

"A guy would be foolish to resist."

His rich tones flowed over her, sparking hope in her chest. "If the weather was nicer, I would've suggested a picnic, but I really don't want to sit on the frozen ground." She walked past him and retrieved a thermos and two travel mugs from her backpack, then faced him again. "However, I did bring hot cocoa. Want some?"

"Sure, sounds great." He smiled at her, then turned back to the water. "Beautiful spot."

"It's my happy place."

"I can see why. It's so peaceful. The rushing water is like nature's symphony." Then he laughed sort of under his breath and shook his head. "Man, that sounded cheesy."

"Cheesy or not, I liked it." She pulled off her mittens and shoved them into her pockets.

The cap wouldn't budge. She tucked it under her arm and twisted with all her strength, but the cap wouldn't budget. Leaning against Cheyenne, she lowered her chin and shook her head. "I can't do this. This is ridiculous."

"What is?"

She waved a finger between them. "This. You and me."

"We're ridiculous?"

"Not we. Me. I'm shaking so much I can't even open this stupid thermos."

Cole moved toward her, took the thermos and set it on the ground. Then he sandwiched her chilly fingers between his warm hands. "What's going on, Macey?"

As if this moment couldn't be humiliating enough, tears welled in her eyes and slid down her cheeks before she could even get her emotions in check. "I'm an idiot, that's what's going on. I imagined this romantic moment of drinking hot cocoa at my favorite spot so I could tell you I was so sorry about what happened at the ball and thank you for saving my family's land and try and figure out where we stood with each other. But now I just feel like there's this giant ball of uncertainty in my stomach and maybe coming here was actually a mistake."

Cole traced the trail of tears with the pad of his thumb. "Macey, breathe."

She pulled her hand free, snatched her mitten out of her pocket and pressed it against her eyes. "Sorry. It's been a whirlwind the past couple of days."

"Well, the good news is, I'm here. And I'm not going anywhere. So relax and tell me what's going on."

Pulling in a deep breath, Macey exhaled, emptying her lungs and pushing out the pent-up anxiety that kept her tossing and turning for the past few nights. She wiped her eyes one final time, then pocketed the mitten once again.

Squaring her jaw, she looked at Cole. His blue eyes shimmered with kindness and the gentle way his thumb stroked her knuckles gave her the courage she needed to express what was in her heart. "I like you, Cole. A lot. No, that's not true." She shook her head.

He frowned. "You don't like me?"

She shook her head, then nodded. She was botching this. "No, I mean, I do like you. A lot. I love you, in fact. There, I said it. I love you."

His lips widened slowly until a grin stretched across his face. He moved closer until he grasped her elbows. His face was so close she could see the flecks of navy in his eyes. "I'm so glad to hear you like me. I'm even happier to know you love me. I love you, too, Macey."

She sighed and pressed her forehead against his. "I wasn't sure how you felt since things fell apart during the ball. I'm so sorry for not listening to you. I was being selfish. After the way your uncle treated you, I didn't need to be a jerk too."

"No, I get it. I planned to tell you everything after the ball. I wanted a perfect evening, but my uncle's unexpected entrance ruined it. But now—just so we're clear…"

He came closer and touched his lips to hers. Her arms looped around his neck as she leaned into him.

Her anxiety melted away like the spring thaw.

She pulled back and rested her head on his shoulder as his arms tightened around her. Then she looked up at him. "I need to tell you something else."

"What else could be better than hearing that you love me?" He cupped his hand around her cheek.

"Don't get mad, but I talked to Wyatt. He's the one who gave me the courage I needed to reach out to you. He said you were out of work right now. I'm so sorry about that, but I'm glad you're not working for your uncle anymore. He's not good for you. I know he's family, but he takes advantage of you. I also wanted you to know—I never have and I never will consider you a charity case. You're one of the strongest men I know, and I'm so proud of you."

"Thank you, Macey. You have no idea what your words mean to me. And I'm not mad at your brother. I'm glad you contacted me. I planned to reach out to you, but I've been packing. The sooner Lexi and I are out of the condo, the quicker we'll be away from my uncle. I'm learning family isn't just through blood but also through love." The wind picked up, ruffling his hair as his eyes turned serious. "I need to tell you something as well, and it may not be what you want to hear."

Macey's stomach sank. He said he loved her, right? She hadn't imagined that.

Whatever he had to say, they'd get through it. Together.

The look of panic on Macey's face had him wishing he could take back his words.

Cole blew out a breath and dragged a hand over his face.

He entwined his fingers through Macey's and gave her hands a gentle squeeze. Then he drew her close and rested his chin on the top of her head. "I meant what I said—I do love you. And I want to see where this goes."

She pulled back. "But?"

"Wyatt invited me to his men's group, and I went last night. Good group of guys. In fact, Heath Walker attends. After losing his ranch, he became a contractor who started his own business. We talked after the meeting, and he invited me to meet him for breakfast. I met with him this morning."

"How'd it go?"

"It went well. We talked about my experience with Crawford Developments, and he offered me the position of being his project manager. He's a small company with a handful of employees, including one of my former foremen. His previous manager just got married and moved away, leaving a hole he needed to fill right away. He's starting a new job of building affordable housing."

Macey's eyes widened as her hands flew to her

mouth. "Cole, that's amazing. Congratulations! I'm so excited for you. You'll be doing exactly what you had dreamed."

He nodded, his jaw tight. "Man, I wish we'd talked yesterday instead of now."

"Why's that?"

"He wants me to oversee the rest of his main job in Durango before we begin building the housing here in Aspen Ridge. The time frame is to have it finished within the next four months."

"Are you moving to Durango?"

He lifted a shoulder. "I'm not sure yet. Either I commute nearly an hour or else I find temporary housing in the city."

"How do you feel about that?"

"I don't mind the city. I just don't want to live there. I love Aspen Ridge, and I want to raise Lexi here. But this job sounds amazing. He offers solid benefits—even better than the ones Wallace offered me."

"I see." Macey bit her lip and toed the snow with the tip of her boot. Then she lifted her eyes. "My dad says it's all about trusting God even when we don't know what's going to happen." She paused and waved a finger between them. "You and me. We're going to work. I know it in my heart. We have some details to figure out. To be honest, I'm not so sure what I want to do with the rest of my life. I just know I want you and Lexi to be a part of it. So if we have to do the long-distance thing for a few months, then I'm game if you are. But if you want to commute, I'm more than willing to help care for Lexi."

Cole's shoulders sagged. He reached for Macey's arms and drew her close to him. He rested his forehead against hers. "I'm so glad to hear you say that. I'm not exactly sure what the next few months will hold, but I do know I want you to be a part of them too."

She stood on tiptoes and brushed a kiss across his lips. "I love you."

"I love you too. And nothing will ever change that." He pressed a kiss to her lips. Taking her hands, he knelt in front of her, snow dampening his knee. "I've known you most of my life, Macey. Even though we haven't even gone on a real date yet, I know I want to spend the rest of my life with you." He pulled a rose-colored velvet box out of his front jeans pocket and opened the lid. "Will you marry me?"

Her hand flew to her mouth as her eyes shimmered. She held out shaky fingers as he lifted the sparkling solitaire from the satin bed and slid it onto her finger.

Perfect fit.

But he had no doubts.

Pushing to his feet, he wrapped her in his arms, lifting her off the ground. "Macey Stone, I promise to stand up for you and spend the rest of my life showing you how much I love you."

"I love you, too, Cole…" She leaned back and gripped his biceps. "I promise to be the one you can lean on. I will be the best mom I can to Lexi…and any other children in our future."

"I like the sound of that." Cole brushed a kiss on her lips.

Macey touched the diamond he'd slid on her finger. "This is the most perfect ring. I can't believe you had it with you. Confident much?"

He laughed, took her hands and kissed her knuckles, then gave them a gentle squeeze. "Actually, I didn't buy that ring. It belonged to my mom. Even though my parents' marriage was cut short by my dad's death, they loved each other very much. When my first wife and I decided to get married, I didn't even consider it for her. Didn't seem like the right fit—maybe that should've told me something. But after I saw you walk down the stairs at your parents' house the night of the ball, I knew you were the one to wear my mother's wedding ring."

Macey cupped his cheek. "Thank you. I will cherish it."

"And I will cherish you." Cole drew her back into his embrace and knew exactly where he belonged—in Macey's arms.

Epilogue

It wasn't that Macey didn't think this day would ever come, but the fact that she was about to marry Cole was more than a dream come true. No matter how cliché it sounded.

Eight months after driving home in that snowstorm, Macey wore her grandmother's wedding dress, which had been altered and updated, and her mother's veil as she clutched her bouquet of wildflowers in one hand and curled her other into the crook of her father's elbow.

Sunlight glinted off the waterfall splashing into the river behind Cole where he stood looking dashing in his light gray suit with her two brothers.

Dressed in shades of soft green, Everly and Mallory, who was finally stateside and able to take leave, preceded her down the makeshift aisle under the grove of lush green trees in full bloom. Lexi and Mia tossed handfuls of flowers as Tanner trailed behind them, looking very bored.

Her eyes connected with Cole's as she forced herself to take steady steps in time to the music. Surrounded by family and a handful of friends, Macey didn't even try to stop the tears that slid out the corners of her eyes. Once she reached Cole, he thumbed them away, then took her hand in his.

For the next fifteen minutes, she tried to focus on the pastor's words, wanting to remember every one. She recited her vows, promising to love, honor and cherish the man standing in front of her. He did the same, then slid the simple wedding band onto her finger.

"By the power vested in me by the state of Colorado, I now pronounce you husband and wife. Cole, you may kiss your bride."

"About time." Cole grinned, then his eyes darkened as he cradled Macey's face in his warm hands. They kissed and sealed their future together.

Then, he touched his forehead to hers. "I love you, Mrs. Crawford."

"I love you too, Mr. Crawford."

A slight tug on her gown pulled Macey's attention away from the man who had stolen her heart. She looked down at Lexi, who wore a cream-colored dress with a lavender tulle skirt. Macey crouched and twirled her finger around one of the ringlets framing Lexi's face. "You look like a fairy princess, Lexi Jane."

She flung her arms around Macey's neck. "You need to teach Daddy how to say my name. He still doesn't get it right."

Still holding on to her new daughter, Macey laughed and looked up at her husband. She shot him a wink. "My pleasure."

"Macey?"

"Yes, sweetheart?"

"Since you married my daddy, does that make you my new mommy?"

Tears warmed the backs of Macey's eyes as she pushed through the thickening in her throat. "Would you like me to be your new mommy?"

Lexi nodded, her smile lighting up her face. "I would like that so much. My daddy is too big for me to take care of all by myself."

Macey pulled the child into her arms, her heart swelling three times its size. "How about we take care of him together?"

"Good idea. Can I call you Mommy?"

Not trusting her voice, Macey nodded, then cast a glance at Cole who brushed his thumb and forefinger over his eyes.

"Yay, I love you, Mommy." Lexi threw her arms around Macey's neck.

"I love you too, princess." Holding on to Lexi's hand, she stood and leaned her head against Cole's shoulder. "If it's okay with you, we need to look into filing paperwork so I can adopt Lexi legally."

Cole dropped a kiss on the top of Macey's head. "It's more than okay with me."

Holding hands, Macey's parents walked up to the three of them. Mom kissed her cheek. "I've said it already, but I'll say it again, you are so beautiful, honey."

"Thanks, Mom. And thank you for loaning me your pearls." Macey fingered the strand of pearls draped around her neck.

"Actually, those were not mine."

"Really? Then where did they come from."

"They belonged to your grandma. Your grandpa had given them to her as a wedding gift. She had given them to Lynetta to wear at her wedding, then Lynetta loaned them to me when I married your dad. She told me to hold on to them until one of you girls got married."

"I loved having a little bit of Grandma and Grandpa with us today. Thank you for allowing us to get married at South Bend."

Dad pulled an envelope from his inside jacket pocket. "Speaking of South Bend—today seems like the best time as any to give this to you."

"What's this?" Her eyes volleyed between them as she took it.

"Open it."

Macey looked at Cole, then slid a manicured nail under the glue flap. She pulled out an official looking letter, scanned it, then gasped. Her hand flew to her mouth. "Are you serious?"

"Absolutely."

Cole frowned. "What's going on?"

Macey handed him the paper, and he read it. "Wow, is this for real?"

Dad chuckled. "You two are a couple of doubters, aren't you?"

"More like overwhelmed."

Dad squeezed her hand lightly. "You've always loved South Bend, so today seemed like the perfect day to give it to you. Take over the old homestead or tear it down and build something new in its place. It's now yours to do as you wish." He lowered his head and whispered in her ear. "Don't worry about your brothers and sisters. They'll get their share in due time."

Tears washed her eyes for like the hundredth time since waking up that morning. "I don't know what to say."

"How about thank you?"

Macey laughed through a blurry haze. "Thank you both. I love you guys. So much."

They pulled her in for a group hug. "We love you too. All three of you." Mom cupped Lexi's face in her hands. "I'm so excited to have another granddaughter."

Bear ambled over to them, hands in his pockets. "Hey, I hate to break up this hugfest, but the photographer needs the bride and groom if we're to get these pictures going."

Lexi ran ahead with Mia and Tanner. Macey and Cole followed them to the archway where they'd exchanged vows moments ago.

The photographer positioned Macey's family around her. As Cole squeezed her hand, she smiled through another sheen of tears.

She had everything she always wanted—a beautiful daughter, a place to call home and a husband who not only rescued her ranch but also rescued her heart.

* * * * *

Dear Reader,

Life doesn't go the way we want, does it? No matter how carefully we plan, something messes with our carefully organized agendas. Then we have to figure out how to deal with those problems. You may have felt like Macey—returning home was a last resort. Perhaps you've felt like Cole—responsible for making your way in the world.

Those lies creep into our heads and block out the Truth God wants us to understand—He created us for relationships. And He puts others in our lives to help us through life's challenges.

When I started this book series, I hadn't visited the area of Colorado where I set the fictional Stone River Ranch. However, when this idea sparked, I trusted God to provide the research resources in order to write this story, especially when life threw constant challenges as I strived to meet my deadline. I completed this book only because of Him.

I hope you enjoyed Cole and Macey's story and look forward to reading more about the Stone family. As each of the Stone siblings walks through their own difficulties, they will learn (as I hope you do too!) God is always present to help them through whatever situations they're facing. Trust the Lord with all your heart and allow Him to direct your paths.

Thank you for reading my books. I'm so blessed by your continued support. I love to hear from my readers, and you can email me at lisa@lisajordanbooks.com.

Embrace His grace,
Lisa Jordan

Get 4 FREE REWARDS!

We'll send you 2 FREE Books plus 2 FREE Mystery Gifts.

FREE
Value Over
$20

Both the **Love Inspired®** and **Love Inspired® Suspense** series feature compelling novels filled with inspirational romance, faith, forgiveness and hope.

YES! Please send me 2 FREE novels from the Love Inspired or Love Inspired Suspense series and my 2 FREE gifts (gifts are worth about $10 retail). After receiving them, if I don't wish to receive any more books, I can return the shipping statement marked "cancel." If I don't cancel, I will receive 6 brand-new Love Inspired Larger-Print books or Love Inspired Suspense Larger-Print books every month and be billed just $6.49 each in the U.S. or $6.74 each in Canada. That is a savings of at least 16% off the cover price. It's quite a bargain! Shipping and handling is just 50¢ per book in the U.S. and $1.25 per book in Canada.* I understand that accepting the 2 free books and gifts places me under no obligation to buy anything. I can always return a shipment and cancel at any time by calling the number below. The free books and gifts are mine to keep no matter what I decide.

Choose one: ☐ **Love Inspired** ☐ **Love Inspired Suspense**
Larger-Print Larger-Print
(122/322 IDN GRHK) (107/307 IDN GRHK)

Name (please print)

Address   Apt. #

City   State/Province   Zip/Postal Code

Email: Please check this box ☐ if you would like to receive newsletters and promotional emails from Harlequin Enterprises ULC and its affiliates. You can unsubscribe anytime.

Mail to the Harlequin Reader Service:
IN U.S.A.: P.O. Box 1341, Buffalo, NY 14240-8531
IN CANADA: P.O. Box 603, Fort Erie, Ontario L2A 5X3

Want to try 2 free books from another series! Call 1-800-873-8635 or visit www.ReaderService.com.

*Terms and prices subject to change without notice. Prices do not include sales taxes, which will be charged (if applicable) based on your state or country of residence. Canadian residents will be charged applicable taxes. Offer not valid in Quebec. This offer is limited to one order per household. Books received may not be as shown. Not valid for current subscribers to the Love Inspired or Love Inspired Suspense series. All orders subject to approval. Credit or debit balances in a customer's account(s) may be offset by any other outstanding balance owed by or to the customer. Please allow 4 to 6 weeks for delivery. Offer available while quantities last.

Your Privacy—Your information is being collected by Harlequin Enterprises ULC, operating as Harlequin Reader Service. For a complete summary of the information we collect, how we use this information and to whom it is disclosed, please visit our privacy notice located at corporate.harlequin.com/privacy-notice. From time to time we may also exchange your personal information with reputable third parties. If you wish to opt out of this sharing of your personal information, please visit readerservice.com/consumerchoice or call 1-800-873-8635. **Notice to California Residents**—Under California law, you have specific rights to control and access your data. For more information on these rights and how to exercise them, visit corporate.harlequin.com/california-privacy.

LIRLIS22R3

HARLEQUIN
PLUS

Try the best multimedia subscription service for romance readers like you!

Read, Watch and Play.

Experience the easiest way to get the romance content you crave.

Start your **FREE TRIAL** at
www.harlequinplus.com/freetrial.